the Moon In You

Alexandria King

& ILLUSTRATED.BY
Leighyah Allen

This book is to all women who have suffered difficult periods without the knowledge of how to make them better.

To my beautiful daughter, mother and father. To my family, both blood and spirit, who light my way and fill my heart. Thank you.

Thank you to Kim Martyn for teaching me in the way she does everyone she meets. For being generous with herself and helping me on my way toward teaching at a young age when my path wasn't yet set.

Our Great Moon Poem

She sings a great song
In your honor

The moon, she sees the light in you
To mirror the spirit inside of you

At the same time she calls to you
While singing a great song of you

It's time for her to shine again
To tell the story for you to hear again

So you see in you what belongs to you
That there is nothing at all wrong with you

To see in you what you already know
That lies in shadow yet to show

That your shining light seen in the day
Is but a flash of your true way

She comes to stay aside your bed
To show you truth inside your head

In your dreams and thoughts and stories
Are carried seeds of many glories

To see with your eyes what only they can see
And the shining light of free, be free

What eyes cannot, what's left for heart
Is where you end and where you start

The moon is here to hear your fear
For you to know she's always near

So you can be who you wish for your own sake
To walk your path and never quake

She sings a song for you tonight
For you to hear of your own light

She sits aside your bed tonight
For you to know it will be alright

The moon, she sees the light in you

Welcome!

Sweethearts, I want you to know how much you are loved, how beautiful you are and how beautiful each of us is. You are the flower that came from the seed that was you. A growing up woman, growing up perfect—just as nature intended.

In this book is everything you need to grow. You are going to be learning about your nature, the moon in you. You'll learn about the magic of women and periods and your naturally perfect beauty. All the topics wild women need to know: how to clean blood stains, all about period feelings, getting to know your private parts by touch, using plant medicine, and the pink and red colors of a period party celebration! You'll learn all about yourself so you can make choices that feel right to you. You'll understand why you're so special and why you need to celebrate yourself.

If you've stumbled onto this book and you're not a girl, read this. You don't need to apologize for reading this or explain yourself. Something inside you needs to know why women are how they are, and this is the best place to start.

After reading you will understand womanhood better, but don't stop there. After you finish this book, pass it on to someone else who needs it, and spend time with women asking questions. We are stronger together.

With gentle loving care for your first period and all the rest to come,

Alexandria King

Illustrations by Leighyah Allen (leighyah.com)
Flower wallpaper painting by Hannah Stone (gohannahstone.com)
Back cover photo by Billie Woods
Editing assistance by Coreen Boucher (lucentedits.com), Wendy Judith and
Kim Martyn

Inside

1. **The Secret•11**
2. **The Unfolding Of Puberty•15**
3. **The Flower Of Life•28**
   Meeting Your Cervix and Vagina•35
4. **The Reproductive Cycle•39**
5. **Moon Wise•52**
   Moon Watching•56
6. **Period Inventions•61**
   Feeling Your Hymen•70
   Making Your Calendar Key•79
7. **Nature's Medicine Cabinet•81**
8. **How Your Mother Got Pregnant•95**
9. **Birth Control•106**
10. **Birth•117**

Author's Note•127
An Epilogue for Mother's Uniting•129
'The Moon In You' Dictionary•133
Wild Medicinal Herbs for Girls
and Women•141
Online Resources•161
Bibliography and Notes•165

Bold words throughout the book appear in the dictionary at the back. Be sure to look them up as you go.

♥ A few words from Leighyah

Hi, I'm Leighyah Allen. I'm fifteen. And this book has been a part of my life since I was eleven. When I was eleven, my mom and I moved across Canada, leaving behind almost everything that everyone thought should have mattered to us. People, I think, thought we were crazy to do something so drastic on what they thought was a whim. But really, nothing is a whim when everything is part of a plan, right? Because there's a plan for us all. It was part of the plan for us to make this book and for me to illustrate, read, and re-read the words my mother wrote. It was also part of the plan for so much to change, so much so, that there's nothing left to do now but grow.

The knowledge in this book will help many people to understand parts of their anatomy that many find shameful. Maybe it will guide you to understand yourself better, maybe it will teach you how to love yourself. Because if you could love yourself the same way you love the pictures of models in magazines, that people tell you you should want to be like, then maybe the next girl who's born won't even think twice about doing the same. But back to the book.

This all started when my mom turned to me and said, "Leighyah, I think I want to move to the West Coast." And I turned to her and asked, "Where on the West

Coast mum?" But she didn't have an answer for me then, nor did she have an answer for me when we landed in the Vancouver airport not three weeks later. When our friends in Vancouver didn't answer our phone calls, we felt then that we should take up the idea of visiting that small Gulf Island called Salt Spring.

So we went across the sea on a tiny ferry boat and landed on the soil of, what to me was, a foreign land. It didn't take us long to get settled and to put down roots. But we would still move around, from place to place, like nomads. Venturing into non-traditional living.

But all the while working on a book for girls, for girls whose only information about their body came from an uncomfortable hour and a half health class that had forty other kids and that was being taught through the fears of the adults teaching them. Classes on abstinence encouraged girls to be 'wholesome' and promoted fears of being a slut. This fear that keeps girls locked down in their body, unable to express themselves.

I feel like even if this book only helps a few girls understand that they're just as special as everyone else, then maybe they could help other girls to feel the same. And that one day, everyone can say with complete truth that everybody and every aspect of every body is completely perfect, even the things other people judge as 'wrong.'

Leighyah

1

The Secret

The secret of life is within you.

The ability to make a baby, if you choose.

Carried in you, Mother Nature, are sacred **seeds** containing information to make new life.

You were born with these seeds. Like an apple that falls from the tree, born with seeds inside to grow more.

Each one contains the genetic code and mystery that has been passed on over generations, for millennia. Gaining wisdom and strength through time they are carried in your body for safekeeping.

In a woman they are called your **eggs** or 'Ovum.' You were born with millions of them, more than you'll need for your entire life. Tiny like the tip of a pin and round like the moon, the moon in you.

Sacred, strong and beautiful, you are the expression of all the information in a seed. And every seed is art, entirely unique in a way that turns out different every single time.

Very closely, follow the structure of your jaw, shoulders, curves of your feet, a strand of your hair. Every part of you is the full blossom of the seed that was you. You are the perfection of Nature.

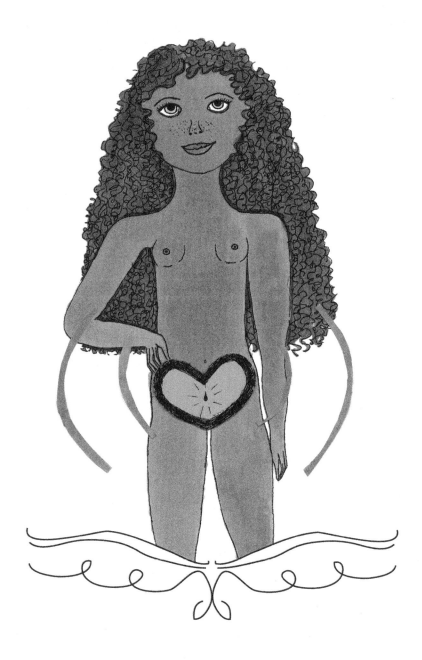

"You are the perfection of nature."

2

The Unfolding Of Puberty

You are becoming a woman. With a woman's body.

When you look in the mirror you can see some changes: growing taller, **breast buds**, skin bumps and new hair everywhere. Changes have been happening for years that you couldn't see, and like a flower that finally opens, your body matures.

Changes happening inside you are felt through tingles of tenderness, feelings and emotions. Many of these changes in your body are caused by **hormones**.

Hormones are what tell the body when to mature and how. The names of hormones are long and sound like the names of chemicals: progesterone (pro-jes-ter-one) and estrogen (es-tro-jen).

Feelings caused by hormones tell your body when to mature and how but feelings are also how you understand your **intuition**. Feelings tell you if you like doing something or not, if you like something or you don't, how you feel about people or the world.

You may prefer to feel only the good feelings, but feelings change like the weather. And to experience all of who you are, you must feel all of the different feelings.

**"You may not have words to express
your feelings but feel them just the
same. Women allow these feelings to
better understand themselves"**

They can be a mix of emotions, such as upset and happiness, or intuition and rage. They can be every mix imaginable.

You may not have words to express your feelings but feel them just the same. Women allow these feelings to better understand themselves.

Over time many people have become uncomfortable with not knowing a lot about themselves. Some people, maybe in your family, have become unfamiliar in their bodies, with their bodies and in sexual relationships. As a result, this may make any of these topics hard for them to feel or talk about at all.

Trust the truth in your feelings; they will show you the way and must be felt to be used as a guide. Your feelings matter more than what anyone else says. No one else knows your emotions or how you feel in your own body, especially now.

"As your body unfolds, allow it."

Your body hasn't grown this fast and had this many changes since you were a little child so go easy on it. While it's quickly changing, you have many parts racing to catch up with one another, and not all at the same time or at the same pace. Some people call this 'growing pains.' This is normal.

The more you give in to the way your body changes, at the pace it changes, the easier time you will have with it emotionally. Accept all the small changes along the way, one change at a time, and one day at a time.

Your body operates on your choices. Choices of what to eat, drink, move and think. Your body is an expression of how you feel in it, how strong, how safe, how courageous or shy. It moves for you, and with you.

This is your beautiful vehicle in life; it needs your love. As your body unfolds, allow it.

First, as your insides change so do the chemicals that make body scent. This scent is all yours, completely unique to you.

A person's scent is used to identify that person. Something we come to like and feel comfortable with when we get to know a person. It reminds us of the uniqueness of them, a memory.

Smells of a body coming out of your pores and underarms like fragrance from a flower. Even though it isn't sweet smelling it has something special about you in it, like a concoction.

If your scent is particularly strong one day and you are feeling pressure to lessen it, just remember that your smell is an expression of your body. Be easy in your thoughts toward yourself.

Since you are what you eat (and feel and think), if you make choices to change any of these things, your body will follow. This includes how you smell.

You are a science experiment for your whole life, the most interesting person you will ever know. Pay attention to any interesting things you notice about yourself, always. If you eat something and notice that you fart a lot, or your teeth turn color or your body scent changes.

When you have the choice of what to eat, it's hard to blame your body for what it does with that food.

Your sweat needs to be expressed, like your feelings and your breath. Don't keep anything in. There are deodorants that take the scent down, but allow the sweat to come out. This is the best choice for your health if you want to use something.

Some pubic hair shapes

Tips & Tricks: Let Sweat Flow

Sweat—let it flow. The body is a system just like the earth that has a flow and balance.

Choose a deodorant instead of an antiperspirant. Antiperspirant blocks the perspiration from coming out of your armpits and, as such, prevents your 'lymphatic system' from emptying through the sweat glands in your armpits. Deodorant will take out the things that make your sweat smelly and still let the sweat come through your pores.

Deodorant crystals are fun to use. Just wet the tip of the crystal and then rub onto your underarms. You may need to re-wet the crystal for the other underarm. Rinse the end to clean after you use it. Again, it is a deodorant and allows the sweat to keep flowing through your body but takes the scent away.

Using soap to wash your underarms also helps keep the scent down as it kills bacteria, and it's the bacteria that make the scent under your arms.

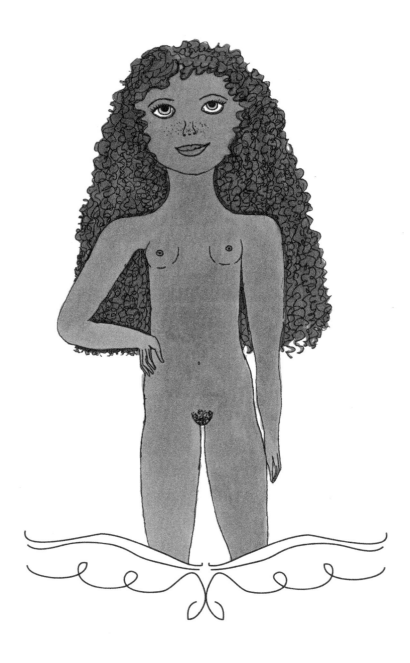

"What makes your breasts grow larger as you mature is the fat that grows around the milk sacs inside your breasts."

New hairs everywhere: you'll see them growing around your **nipples**, on your pubic bone and possibly on your face and under your arms, amongst other places. Hairs may grow anywhere there is skin, in any pattern, in any color, in any shape.

Pubic hairs are the hairs that grow on and around your pubic bone and your **Vulva**. It may or may not look like your mothers or other grown women you've seen. It may also be a different type of hair: curly, wavy or straight and/or a different color.

Often it starts on top of your pubic bone and grows down and around your Vulva. Slowly over time the amount of hair you have increases making a bigger area of pubic hair, as you become a grown woman.

Breast buds are developing. Firm balls under each nipple are growing, tender to the touch.

They may not grow at the same time or even at the same speed and can look the same, be slightly or a lot different. A different shape or size is usual. Breasts, like everything else, will change through your life. So not only is there no one way to be, there's no one way to stay.

The color of your **areola**, the area around your nipple, will darken in color, deepening. Just watch the perfection of you and your colors, shapes and feelings.

If you touch or play with your nipples, they may crimple and harden. They are sensitive to your touch.

Breasts are made to be able to feed a newborn baby and sense pleasure—as your whole body can. Slowly, inside your breasts, small milk glands are starting to form in case you have a baby. They won't be fully developed and be able to fill with milk until after a baby is born. The milk will come out through tiny holes, which you don't have yet, in your nipples.

During **puberty**, the time when your body blossoms and matures before having your first **period**, some wet liquid may come out of your breasts through your nipples that is white or yellow in color. This can also happen in the nipples of newborn babies shortly after birth.

What makes your breasts grow larger as you mature is the fat that grows around the milk sacs inside your breasts. The fat is used to protect the sacs. Regardless of the amount of fat, all milk sacs will provide enough milk for babies to drink.

You may see bumps around your areola in no particular order or pattern. When and if the time comes for you to breast-feed, small amounts of oil will come out of these bumps to make your areola and nipple less dry when there's milk coming out of them all the time. The soft skin of the nipple and areola need the oil to moisturize.

As your breasts grow you may be interested in wearing a bra. Be sure to find one that fits comfortably. You can also try wearing fitted tank tops or undershirts.

Be curious as to how you change. Watch and touch your body, sensing it to see how you feel in it. As it is always changing, you may notice new changes from one day to the next.

Tips & Tricks: Bra Fitting

To get a proper fitting bra, here is how you will find the size that fits.

What you will need: a measuring tape long enough that you could wrap it around your shoulders. Look for a soft one in a sewing kit. Whatever you find will work though.

You have to take two measurements, your breast or 'bust' size and your 'band.'

First your bust. Wrap the measuring tape around your

"Watch and touch your body, sensing it to see how you feel in it."

back and under your arms around your rib cage, then, bring the measuring tape around to the front just under your breasts. Adjust your tape so it's snug, not tight, and read the measurement. This is your measurement but because bras are made with a certain sizing system, if it's an odd number, round down to the nearest even number. Write that down.

To measure your band, again put the measuring tape at your back and pull it around to the fullest or biggest part of your breast in the front. Make sure you can breathe easy—this isn't a corset. You want to take deep breaths while holding the measuring tape. It needs to be fitted, which means a measurement that you can breathe in and that isn't loose either. Round up to the nearest 'whole' even number if the number is a half-inch. Write that down too.

Then do a simple subtraction—band minus bust. So the measurement from under your breasts minus the measurement of the largest part of your bust.

You will get a number from 0-6 and onward. Each of these numbers is represented as the LETTER in the bra size i.e. A36. A is 1, B is 2, C is 3 and so on. If you

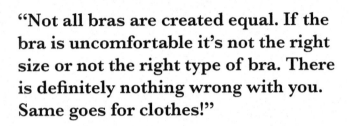

"Not all bras are created equal. If the bra is uncomfortable it's not the right size or not the right type of bra. There is definitely nothing wrong with you. Same goes for clothes!"

are less than 1, you would be a AA. So the letter you got, beside the measurement rounded to the even number is your bra size.

Not all bras are created equal. If the bra is uncomfortable, it's not the right size or not the right bra. There is definitely nothing wrong with you. The bra may have been made wrong, but you are not made wrong.

Stretch marks are lines that may be darker or lighter than your usual skin color with a slightly different texture. This is the result of a growing body. Should you have them, they are common and blend in more over time. How you get them is often a result of genetics and how elastic your skin is. They appear natural.

If you find your skin itchy as stretch marks are happening, use a natural or mild type of moisturizer: the more natural the better. Do your research.

Pimples and skin marks will come and go. When you

make changes to what you eat, take notice from week to week how this affects your skin. In time it subsides because nothing lasts forever.

Your hips may widen while everything inside them is maturing. Your reproductive system is inside, a system of parts inside you that work together in being able to create life.

Your first period is the sign that your body and your reproductive system have mostly matured and is close to the end of puberty, or your unfolding.

3

The Flower Of Life

When looking at your reproductive system, the first thing you see is hair growing on your pubic bone or '**Mound of Venus**.' You can feel the bone underneath the hair.

The hair goes all the way under, back toward your bum. It's hard to look down and see everything. You can use a mirror so you can see your Vulva underneath.

The Vulva is your genitalia on the outside of your body. It's like a flower, delicate, and unfolds like flower petals.

Your Vulva is very sensitive to thought, sight and touch. She feels everything. Feel with your hands to see the un-seeable. You'll learn that not everything feels the way it looks.

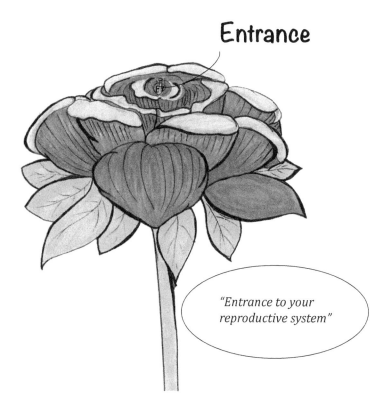

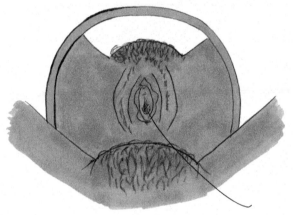

Entrance

"Your Vulva unfolds like flower petals."

If you press too hard, you won't feel as much as when you use a light touch. Your Vulva likes soft strokes, warmth or an even more delicate pressure, like a drop of water. The most gentle of things helps it to unfold.

The large 'lips' on the outside are called the **Labia Majora**. They look most like petals. They can be wavy and ruffled or smooth and straight, or anything in between. They are as unique to you as the curves on your face.

Tips & Tricks: Softly Touching Your Vulva

Like the unfolding of a rose bud, your Vulva needs love and time to allow it to unfold. To feel pleasure, you can lick your finger or put saliva onto your finger and very softly explore what touching yourself feels like. Explore the sensation around your inner and outer labia, around and on your clitoris. See if you can find all of your parts by touch without looking. You'll know when it's time to touch yourself; you'll have a physical sensation when it's welcomed. Go with your intuition and feelings.

Pubic hair usually stays on the outside of the Labia Majora or the 'bigger lips.'

"Like an iceberg shows only a small piece of itself above the water, your Clitoris is mostly inside your body where you can't see."

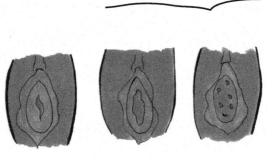

Possible hymen shapes

Going inward from that are a smaller pair of lips that don't have hair and are even more delicate, soft and sensitive: your **Labia Minora**.

At the top of the Vulva, there is a tent of skin that looks like a triangle over top of a little bump. If you gently pull the skin up toward your Mound of Venus, you will reveal your **Clitoris**, the most sensitive part of your genitals.

To touch it with a finger is even too much. It prefers that, if you use a finger, for the finger to be moist. You can also touch on top of the hood of skin leaving it covered and gently move it around this way. Because it's so sensitive, using the cover may help to use just enough pressure.

Like an iceberg shows only a small piece of itself above the water, your Clitoris is mostly inside your body where you can't see. That 'small' Clitoris has many nerve endings to make it super sensitive.

Underneath this is the opening that pee comes from. It's called your **Urethra** and leads to your bladder where pee is held.

You have three separate openings. One is for pee, one is the entrance to your vagina and the third is your **anus** where poo comes out.

Your Vulva is made of layers of soft tissue and muscle, some that you can see and some underneath that you can't, connecting through each other and to many parts of your genitalia in a beautiful web, making your Vulva and all connecting parts a beautiful space of sensitivity and strength.

Not one part is more important than the next. Not one part with less beauty than the others. Working perfectly together.

This soft connecting tissue leads you to see the opening of your Vagina. If you gently part your inner lips with your fingers by separating them to the sides, you can look inside a little. You may see the Hymen if there is one depending on the position you're in while looking.

The **Hymen** is a thin layer of skin you were born with that covers your vaginal opening. Over time the hymen stretches and holes or spaces are created in it. How a hymen looks as a result is always different.

It may continue to open over time or with lots of physical activity leaving little left even before something is inserted into your vagina for the first time. Inserting a tampon or having sex for the first time may also push the rest of the hymen out of the way until it isn't noticeable. The breaking apart of the skin can be very uncomfortable or completely unnoticeable.

Your vagina is a canal, a passage that leads to your **uterus**. It is a little bit longer than your longest finger most of the time and can extend longer when you feel good.

It's a soft moist place like the inside of your cheek.

When inserting a finger, your **Vagina** doesn't go straight up. Your vaginal canal changes often and in one month can go from being dry and smooth to lush, soft and mushy with lots of slippery liquid.

Like a snail goes to hide in its shell, to protect its delicate self, your Vulva is sensitive to everything including your thoughts.

Your body and your vagina are always responding to your feelings and changing their look, size and feel. A body is never the same, always changing. It's alive.

At the top of your vaginal canal is your **cervix**, the door to your uterus. Your cervix is a gem. Looking similar in shape to a donut, with a very small slit or hole in the middle. Small enough for period blood to come through but not big enough to put your finger through.

UNDERWEAR CHECK

You may have already noticed some white stuff on your underwear or when you wiped after going pee. This is most likely **cervical fluid**. Made from your cervix, it travels down your vagina and out. It can have many textures, from clear and slippery like egg whites to white or yellowish and clumpy.

)EXERCISE(
Meeting Your Cervix and Vagina

1. The first time you insert your finger into your vagina should be a special moment. Give yourself time and privacy to be with yourself for this special moment.

2. In a comfortable position with your knees apart and your vagina open, wet your finger with saliva so it can slide in comfortably: the warmer and wetter the better.

3. When you first touch your finger to the outside of your vagina become familiar with how soft and sensitive it is. This will tell you how to touch your-

self. You can open the feelings in your vagina by loving you and that part of you. Gently search and touch around the outside along your lips and between folds.

4. Feel every bit of it. Let it be a discovery of pleasure.

5. You can touch the entrance of the vagina and, if there is slippery cervical liquid coming out, you can use this to get your finger wetter so that it moves around easier.

6. Slowly insert your finger, using your senses as a guide. If you don't feel ready, stop. If and when you wish, try it again another time when you feel more comfortable.

7. As your finger goes in, know that the vagina heads up and then slightly towards your bum. You'll feel soft squishiness hugging your finger as you go in.

8. If you sense your hymen when you enter your vagina, lightly feel around.

9. If your body is ready and you would like to touch it, go ahead and explore. It stretches and is soft tissue.

10. If the hymen doesn't take up too much room at the entrance of your vagina, see how much space there is to put your finger through comfortably. See how it feels to touch near it or around it.

11. Giving yourself as much time as you need: there is only one pace and that's yours.

12. If you feel comfortable, keep exploring and head up.

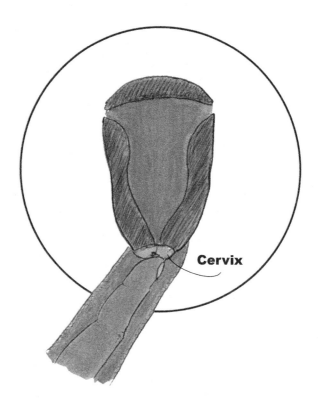

13. Your cervix is just before the end of the vagina. It's like a big nub sticking out just before the end of the vagina. Using your finger as a measuring stick, it's likely that with your longest finger fully inserted you'll be feeling it.

14. However, your cervix changes all month long so don't feel discouraged if you didn't feel it. Just keep trying, it may have been hiding or not obviously sticking out that day.

Your cervix is at the bottom of your uterus, and through the small entrance in the middle of your cervix is the doorway to your uterus, womb or 'baby room.' The place where your period blood comes from and where a baby grows. The top of the uterus is approximately two inches below your belly button and can stretch up to 1000 times its original size in order to grow a baby inside.

There are two tubes or arms that connect your uterus to your ovaries. These are your **fallopian tubes**.

Your ovaries, one at the end of each tube, are where your eggs are stored. They have been kept safe through time in each woman so they may get pregnant. The ovaries are the place where magic happens, where the eggs go through a process of maturing called Ovulation. Much like puberty when your body matures, the egg goes through its own process, its own cycle.

The Reproductive Cycle

Your reproductive system is within you.

It works like all of your body's systems— miraculously on its own. Like the digestive system, which processes food without you lifting a hand.

Everything from your 'Flower of Life' is a part of your reproductive system. This system works to be able to grow life and carry it within you, to be able to become pregnant.

Hormones instruct your reproductive system how to work together like a cooperative assembly line. And as your body matures, your first period starts near the end of puberty.

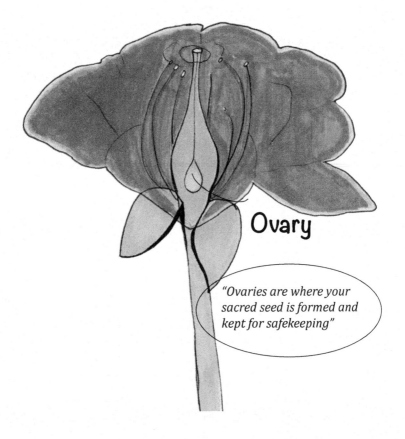

Ovary

"Ovaries are where your sacred seed is formed and kept for safekeeping"

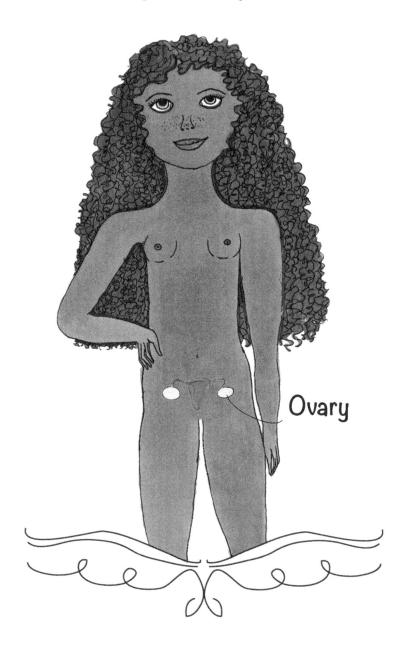

Ovary

"Your feelings are your greatest teacher."

With it begins your 'reproductive cycle,' of which your period is a part of.

The reproductive cycle and system may sound complicated as it's happening inside of you where you can't see, but it's easy for your body, like walking and chewing gum, just a few things going on at the same time.

This cycle starts and ends continuously, on and on, around like the seasons moving into one another throughout a year. Your cycle is a monthly process that your body goes through in order to prepare your body for a possible pregnancy each and every month from the time you have your first period until your last.

Although you may not yet feel ready, your period is a sign that you will likely be able to become pregnant when and if you choose. Not all women are able to become pregnant. Some try and don't become pregnant right away; sometimes months later, it happens.

Every cycle your reproductive system will carry a seed in you and make a place for it to stay and grow or to dissolve in the tube.

Your Reproductive System

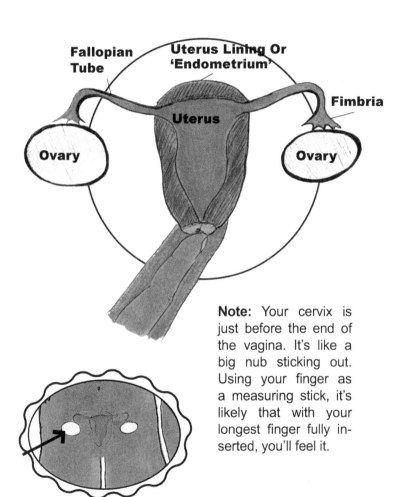

Note: Your cervix is just before the end of the vagina. It's like a big nub sticking out. Using your finger as a measuring stick, it's likely that with your longest finger fully inserted, you'll feel it.

The Reproductive System In You!

Tips & Tricks: Imagination Cycle

The images you're about to see are sketches of what your reproductive system looks like inside of you. First imagine where your reproductive system is in your body. Place your hands about where it is. Imagine how it feels.

Hint: The top of your uterus is a short distance below your belly button and each **ovary** *is about the size of a small walnut without the shell on.*

If you want get creative and use body paint to draw on your reproductive system and as you go through this chapter, imagine your own reproductive system inside you go through a cycle like a movie. Feeling it happen.

Ovulation: The Birth of An Egg

It starts with an egg.

One egg, one sacred seed containing the information to make life will mature ahead of the rest.

About once a month, your eggs will go through a process of maturing in your ovaries. This is called **Ovulation**. Many eggs will be maturing in both ovaries, but one egg will be the most mature of the bunch to make the egg journey for this cycle.

There is no exact order of which ovary goes first or in what order. It could be in either ovary, just the first most mature egg will go.

What Your Reproductive System Does in One Month

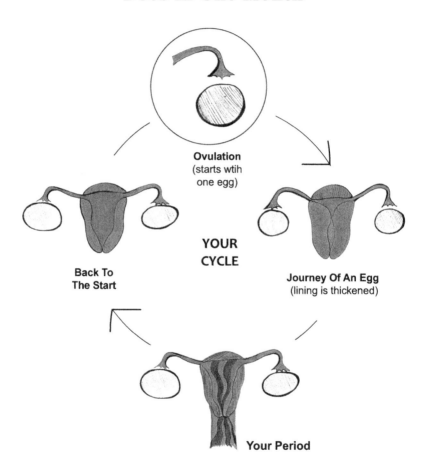

Ovulation
(starts wtih
one egg)

**YOUR
CYCLE**

**Back To
The Start**

Journey Of An Egg
(lining is thickened)

Your Period

It will explode from the ovary that it's in and be caught by the wavy fingers or '**fimbria**' at the end of the fallopian tube. The egg will be drawn into the fallopian tube to travel toward the uterus.

Your egg, round like the moon and tiny like the tip of a needle, is attractive, like a magnet drawing energy toward it by simply being. This is the energy of a womb, a woman and a moon.

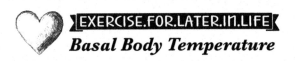

]EXERCISE.FOR.LATER.IN.LIFE[
Basal Body Temperature

Your **basal body temperature** is the lowest temperature you have within 24 hours. From a few days before Ovulation until around the end of your period, your basal body temperature is higher than it is for the rest of your cycle.

To do a temperature experiment, take your temperature every day for one complete cycle (when you begin having your cycle regularly of course) at the same time every day; first thing in the morning is best. Keep a record.

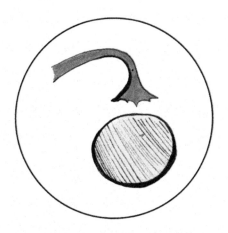

UNDERWEAR CHECK

Ovulation is the easiest time to become pregnant, when your cervical fluid is clear and slippery like egg whites. It also makes your vagina feel the best, the most comfortable, slippery in texture and feeling good when you move around. Cervical fluid helps sperm enter through your cervix in search of an egg when you have sex. Read more about this in 'Chapter 8: How Your Mother Got Pregnant.'

The Journey Of An Egg

The egg's journey is through the fallopian tube, heading toward the uterus. The egg is helped along the way by tiny hairs in the fallopian tube like little hands and by clear fluid that helps and protects the delicate egg.

Meanwhile, in your uterus, the lining or **endometrium** is being prepared with a thick layer of nutritious period blood. This is the period of building.

If a sperm fertilized your egg, the egg would then be planted in your uterus lining to grow.

Period blood is a mixture of blood cells, mucus, cervical discharge and some blood. This combination makes the

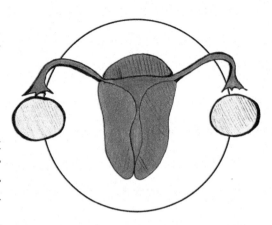

most nutritious mixture for a beginning baby to be planted.

Breasts

In the week before your period, your breasts may get bigger and become tender. They are retaining (holding onto) water and anticipating pregnancy. If you were to have a baby, the milk glands in your breasts would make your milk. The tenderness should relax after your period comes.

UNDERWEAR CHECK

Getting closer to your period, cervical fluid gets thicker in texture, like thick white or yellowish yogurt.

Your Period

If the egg has not been fertilized, the endometrium or lining starts breaking apart and shedding (bleeding).

The blood comes out naturally and easy. It may contain clots or bumpy pieces and may be any shade of red imaginable from bright red to dark brown. All is normal.

Its red is a treasure.

Although it's hard to tell how much comes out each period, it's only between a few tablespoons and a half a cup in total. It appears more because of all the other things in a period blood mixture and because it's red!

Your body is always making a new lining. Having your period is like a blood refresher: old blood out and new blood made.

Your period is an end to a great story. When an egg hasn't been fertilized and the body knows there is no pregnancy, it gets rid of your period blood to start all over again, ready for a new cycle.

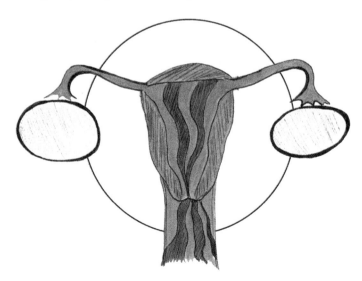

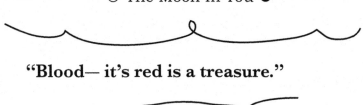

"Blood— it's red is a treasure."

Your First Period

Your first period is your period story, unlike anyone else's. A prize and present, it may turn out to be moving and emotional or you may hardly notice it.

It may come at any time of the day or night. You may have just a little spot of blood or a full period that lasts anywhere from a few days to a week. On average, a girl could get her first period between the ages of 8 and 16.

Period Shame

The only thing dirty about your period is shame— blood is clean. Periods have been made to be shameful. Everyone knows it happens to all women, and most women don't leave any evidence that they have a period at all. Begin to be shameless in your house by not hiding it.

Begin with leaving a little bit of blood or 'love' showing in the wastebasket instead of pushing it down or with leaving a bit in the toilet. If any family members express concern, remind them that although it may be uncomfortable to be reminded that you have a period, there is nothing to fear. This is one small way to become shameless.

Back To The Start

It is a fresh start and new beginning. Your basal body temperature is going back down and likely you will feel like your body has become more still and refreshed.

You will start Ovulating again soon, and so, the cycle continues.

UNDERWEAR CHECK

At this point, there isn't much cervical fluid, if any at all, and your vagina is pretty dry.

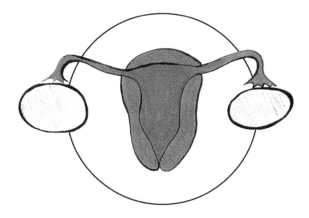

5

Moon Wise

Your cycle is the journey of one egg, the moon in you.

The moon is a she, and she is quiet, subtle energy circling around the earth.

It takes 28 days for a moon to go from being 'new' when you can't see her, completely covered in shadow, to round and 'full' when you can see the whole thing bright in the sky to 'new' again. This 28 days is called a moon cycle.

She is a mirror for women's cycles. A woman's reproductive cycle is about the same length as a moon cycle.

The moon shows us a lot about constant change. She is a natural optical illusion appearing differently in the

"The moon is a she."

sky but is always whole, always her. Like the moon you are always changing, always showing a different side of you.

A girl's or woman's cycle, unlike the moon, can change quite a bit in length. It may be as short as 14 days or not come at all some months; it may be as long as 34

"Like the moon you are always changing, always showing a different side of you."

days or come twice a month. The 28 day moon cycle is an average length of women's cycles, but your cycle may come and go as it pleases.

Tips & Tricks:
Calculate How Long Your Period Is

Count from the first day of your period to the next first day of your period. If your period starts on January 1 and the next period starts on January 26, you had a 26-day cycle. If the period after January 26 starts on February 18, that cycle is 23 days. January has 31 days.

Moon Time

The changing moon that magically reflects our cycle was also a timekeeper for people before calendars. The word 'month' came from the word 'moon.' A month was created to mark how long a moon took to go through one cycle.

Weeks were made to further separate time based on the four main phases of the moon cycle, making four weeks in a month. A year came from the cycle of the earth around the sun. One cycle of the earth turning around the sun makes a year, passing through each season once: spring, autumn, winter and summer.

To track where the months were through the seasons, they named moons after things that reminded them of that specific time. A 'Harvest Moon' in October during the time of the harvest, or a 'Pink Moon' in April when the herb 'moss pink' came out.

Once in a 'Blue Moon' became what people see as the second moon in a month, but it was originally the fourth full moon in a season that usually only has three.

A blue moon may look blue but isn't actually blue. Like seeing something through a camera lens, the color of the moon stays the same, but the lens through which we see it changes.

Since months and calendars don't accurately follow the length of the moon cycle any more, there are occasionally more moons in a year than there are months. With about 28 days a moon cycle and 365 days a year, there may be 13 moons in 12 months. This is one reason you may have two periods in one month.

EXERCISE
Moon Watching

The first and most important part of this exercise is to spend a couple minutes at night observing the moon.

"Periods have been known as a sacred time to sit and digest your emotions..."

That is it. Watch it closely as you would watch a plant growing or a cloud moving. Spend a moment with it, a connection.

Through one 'moon cycle' or month, observe the moon as many nights as you can. Write down any observations about its size and shape and about any feelings you have. Much like 'Recording Your Period Changes,' keep a log entitled 'Observations of My Moon.' Keep your findings of period changes and the moon together on the same calendar or in the same diary. You can take mental notes but keeping a log and writing down changes allows you to see patterns when you read over them later on.

The Moon and Water

For hundreds of years, people have admired her magic, a controller of earth's water. Like a huge magnet in the sky, she pulls and releases the water.

Watch the ocean as she draws the water toward her. The water goes out. Little shells left behind, waiting for the water to come back and wash over them. The tide goes out.

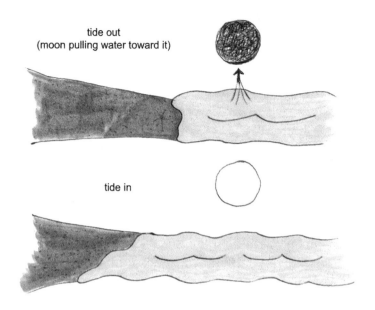

When the water comes back to cover them, we know the moon has moved away and released her magnet-like pull. The tide comes back in.

Period Time

Periods have been known as a sacred time to sit and digest your emotions, a time to allow Mother Nature to take her course.

Your period time is not like the rest of your cycle; it's special and has a special feeling to it.

This period of time, your period, moon flow, menstruation, has remained a mystery to most people. As you have periods month after month, notice the little things that make it different. You'll feel rounder, bigger and fuller in your womb or belly area. You may feel yourself glowing or radiating out of your skin through your whole self. Warmer as your basal body temperature is higher.

It is a time of self-care and a time for reflection.

It is a time to make plans and express your feelings. Write them down if you have to. A time to do your hair, wrap up in a warm blanket, make things, create, write, read, sing, love yourself, share wisdom or spend time with girlfriends. Spend time caring for your body with vitamins and herbal tea, nourishing yourself.

Allow yourself to feel your period, warm, like your skin is expanding and breathing. Let your body unfold by wearing comfy clothes. Play music to yourself. Appreciate what your body looks like and how your emotions change. Listen to your body to find out what makes yourself feel good in your body.

Your feelings are right; use them as a guide. The process of becoming a woman within requires you to listen to your body always, to learn from it, and like clockwork, you will begin to unfold in a way known only to yourself. By listening this way you will feel more sure of yourself and be able to take action on your feelings.

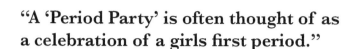

"A 'Period Party' is often thought of as a celebration of a girls first period."

Live as if you are a part of nature, flowing and changing. Live like a wild woman passing through the trees and marking your territory for all to see. Demonstrate what it's like to live as a woman. Your period is destiny— a reminder of your nature.

A special part of period history includes menstrual huts, or red tents, which were a place that women would gather and spend time together while on their periods. Being nourished with plant nutrients, warmth and the warmth of company, creating and making beautiful things, sharing stories and one's innermost thoughts—together. Being stronger together and standing taller with each other. Being womanhood.

Create your own 'red tent' or something like it. Create a vision of womanhood that you dream about and that makes you excited to become a woman. If you feel it, it's possible for your life.

Period Parties

A Period Party is usually a celebration of a girl's first period. It could also be used to celebrate the period of any woman who did not yet celebrate their first period. Or even celebrate any period of any woman, any time of the year.

It looks much like a red birthday party— also known as a 'red party.'

You may throw a party or give a gift to a friend when she has her first period or even for your own mother or any woman you know. Great gifts may include red flowers or red fruit; a pomegranate, rose or something that symbolizes womanhood to you.

Period Inventions

A period invention or product is used to catch or soak up blood so a woman can walk around instead of sitting in one place while the flow happens.

Over time women have explored different ways of experiencing periods. Right now it's time for a refreshing change, a new way to experience our period, to have an enlightening, freeing experience, something new to us. You won't know what you like best unless you try a few things first.

Over time we have come to rely on period "stuff," like pads and tampons, to make the period experience. A period experience is much more than that. Much more than what we use, but if we're choosing something, make it good. Periods happen without much worry about stuff. When you learn that period items are used

"Use natural or organic period items. Your natural body has an easier time with things that are natural in the world."

to catch blood, you find out you can use pretty much any piece of nice absorbent cloth that feels good on your skin and brings a glow to your cheeks.

There are many different types of disposable or 'one use only' period items. Disposable items are made mostly by companies to make waste and money. The most commonly available are pads and tampons.

Disposable items are also made to be convenient, to throw away evidence that your period happened and to stay 'clean.' Little do most women know that a period is clean. Period blood as talked about in Chapter 4 is the combination of nutrients perfect to support the growing of new life and can even be used as a fertilizer to help plants grow.

There are reusable period items such as menstrual cups or cloth pads which allow women to become more intimate and familiar with their own period and period blood.

Use only what brings you joy and lets you feel good,

like a princess that has things made for her pleasure. Remember to choose for pleasure, not only accept what is easily available.

Choosing What To Use

Period items take time to test so start the process now.

This section includes experiments for each type of period item. Test them to find out how they work and what they're all about.

The Vulva and Vagina are sacred, delicate and soft. When trying items, make sure to listen to your body; it knows best.

Choosing How To Experience Your Period

Become a Period Inventionary! Dream up your perfect way of experiencing your period or a new period invention. Have a picture in your mind of the very best situation you can imagine, feelings and all. We need to keep this picture so that we can have as positive a cycle as possible.

The Making of A Good Period Invention

What's good for you is good for the world. Your body, like the world, is alive and whatever you put in one spot affects your whole body.

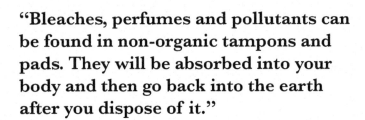

"Bleaches, perfumes and pollutants can be found in non-organic tampons and pads. They will be absorbed into your body and then go back into the earth after you dispose of it."

Organic Vs. Non-Organic

Your natural body has an easier time with things that are natural in the world.

Bleaches, perfumes and pollutants like dioxin and chlorine can be found in non-organic tampons and pads. They will be absorbed into your body and then go back into the earth after you dispose of it. They may also irritate your skin.

An organic box will mention qualities like 'organic,' '100% cotton,' 'not bleached' or 'chlorine free.' Non-Organic items will often be sprayed with chemicals, dyed with bleaches and made from nylon/cotton blend. Look for clearly labelled packages. Yes, they cost a bit more, but it's worth it.

Disposable Pad Mountain

If you use only disposable items, from your first period

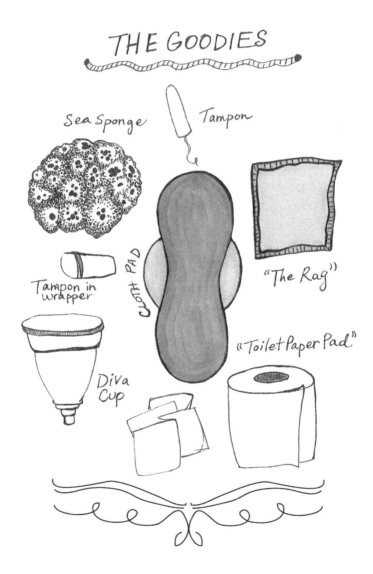

THE GOODIES

Sea Sponge

Tampon

Tampon in wrapper

CLOTH PAD

Diva Cup

"The Rag"

"Toilet Paper Pad"

to the time you have your last period, 11,000 pads will have been thrown away. Depending on if you used organic brands or, non-organic, it will either take 12, 000 years to decompose or for non-organic, take a whopping 200,000 years. Where will you be in 200,000 years?

The Disposable Pad

There are two main shapes that pads come in, wings or no wings, and many lengths and thicknesses. Small and thin are great to wear when you don't bleed much or to wear in preparation for your period coming soon. Super thick are good for when you're bleeding more and need something to wear overnight.

Pads are worn on the inside of your underwear to catch blood. Disposables have two sides, one that is soft and absorbent and the other is sticky and plastic. The sticky part sticks to the underwear. They are worn once and then thrown away. Change them every 4-6 hours or as frequently as is needed.

The disposable pad has been known to retain heat and give some women a rash. With the warmth and wetness of your vagina and blood, the plastic on the bottom of the pad doesn't let the blood through and also doesn't let air through.

Experiment: The Pad Pour

To understand how a pad works, play with one. Well,

two actually, one organic and one non-organic. Soak them in water, stick them to something and think of as many ways to use a pad other than for a period.

Tips & Tricks: Toilet Paper Pad

To make a 'Toilet Paper Pad,' just take a piece of toilet paper about the length of your arm and fold it in half a couple times until it's a bit shorter than a real pad. Try to place the toilet paper pad in between your legs so it sticks a little to the moistness of your Vulva. This will help keep it in place. If there isn't enough fluid to stick it to, it may shift around and fall out.

The Tampon

A tampon is like a compact pad or little sponge that is inserted into the vagina to absorb period blood. Tampons come in different thicknesses but are made in the same style. You can get tampons either with or without an applicator. An applicator is the extra piece of plastic or cardboard attached to a tampon so a woman can insert a tampon without having to touch her vagina.

At the bottom of the tampon is a string that hangs outside of your vagina so you can pull it out when you're finished using it. This is to make it easier to take out so you don't have to go searching for it with your fingers.

Tampons are best used during the daytime and when you have enough blood flowing to be absorbed. When you have a light flow or little fluid coming out, the tampon will just absorb the natural moisture inside your vagina making it uncomfortable to put in and take out. When not bleeding much, it's better to use a small pad until you're bleeding more or until you stop bleeding.

Remember, a tampon can't get lost in your vagina: it can't fit through your cervix, and your vagina comes to an end just past your cervix.

Experiment: The Tampon Test

To find out the difference between organic and non-organic tampons, soak them each in a clear jar and observe.

If the non-organic tampon is made of nylon, you may be able to see little hairs on the sides. When you use a nylon tampon, the little hairs pull at the sides of your vagina increasing the possibility of small tears on your vaginal walls. Soaking them also allows you to see how much water they can absorb.

Using A Tampon For The First Time

Use a tampon only if it feels comfortable to you. Your first time using a tampon is special—give it some time. It is a rite of passage, entering into your vagina or going through your vaginal entrance. There is a word in Sanskrit called **'Yoni'** to describe your vaginal entrance meaning 'entrance to the divine.' That is exactly what it is.

This first entrance by something outside of you should not be overlooked. Tampons are often used with no

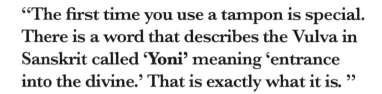

"The first time you use a tampon is special. There is a word that describes the Vulva in Sanskrit called 'Yoni' meaning 'entrance into the divine.' That is exactly what it is. "

thought or ceremony as the sacredness is overlooked in our bodies, in our society, our culture and in our homes.

The importance is not overlooked with you right now, as you consider your first passing with the thought and love it needs.

It's best to try using tampons after you've had your very first period, and a few more after that! You want to get to know what your period looks like, the color of your blood and how much comes out. If you use a tampon right off the bat you won't have a clear picture in your head of what your period looks like.

When choosing your first tampon, choose a slim size. This will be easier to insert. Organic is also particularly important when using tampons as they are inside you and in a moist area that absorbs easily.

To prepare for using a tampon, first do the exercise *'Meeting Your Cervix and Vagina'* in "The Flower of Life' chapter.

Your vagina should be moist and relaxed to use a tampon and your hands clean. Your body, open.

There has to be enough fluid in your vagina that the tampon can slide in so best to try this when you're on your period. If your vagina is too dry, it will be harder to insert it and uncomfortable for your vagina. If the absorbent tampon doesn't have much to soak up, it will soak up the little that is there, leaving your vagina with no moisture.

)EXERCISE(
Feeling Your Hymen

You may have introduced yourself to your hymen in the exercise 'Meeting Your Cervix and Vagina' in the chapter 'The Flower of Life.'

Becoming more familiar with your vaginal canal will make it easier on your body to accept inserted period items.

To prepare your vagina before using a tampon or Diva Cup, you may want to begin with inserting your finger into your vagina, slowly and kindly feeling your hymen if there is one. This will help you to see how much room there is for a tampon to enter.

Go slow with inserting anything for the first time and every time after that, including tampons. This helps every part of your vagina slowly adjust to the thing being inserted. The vagina is all stretchy muscle and knows your feelings. When you are happy to try something and take it slow, it opens up to gradually make room. Likewise, it closes in unhappiness.

Inserting A Tampon <u>Without</u> An Applicator

When using a tampon, use a mirror, go slow, push gently but firmly towards the small of your back/waist. Use a small/light tampon on day one.

Unravel the string from the bottom and put your finger in the nook at the bottom of the tampon while holding onto the tampon with your other finger or fingers. Any way that works will work.

Tips & Tricks: Wetting A Tampon

> You can moisten the end of the tampon by putting saliva on it or by wetting it on your tongue before you insert it in your vagina. You can also try putting oil, like olive or grapeseed, on the end.

Slowly insert it into your vaginal opening. You have to slip it firmly in—our vagina is not a hole! It should go far enough that the first half of your finger is curved in your vagina.

Push the tampon past the bump, which is the first two to three inches inside your vagina and is far enough to sit comfortably. If it doesn't go in far enough, it will feel very uncomfortable, and you obviously feel it, almost like it might come out. If it's in far enough and not disturbing your hymen, you won't be able to feel it at all and it will be comfortable.

"Hand washing is the best way to clean bloodstains. Remember to use cold water and rinse as soon as possible."

Inserting A Tampon <u>With</u> An Applicator

Again, if you are using this for the first time, find an applicator and tampon that is the smallest, thinnest variety.

After taking the wrapping off, there should be a top and bottom portion to the cardboard or plastic applicator. The bottom piece is pushed into the top piece and the tampon pops out at the top. The string is at the bottom.

Slowly insert it into your vaginal opening. Make sure you aren't pushing too hard and everything is comfortably sliding in.

When the first half of the tampon is inside, press the bottom portion into the top; this slides the tampon higher. You may have to use two hands. The applicator will be left in your hand.

If it doesn't go in far enough, it will feel very uncomfortable, and you obviously feel it, almost like it might come out. If it's in far enough and not disturbing your hymen, you won't be able to feel it, and it will be comfortable.

You can flush cardboard applicators but not plastic. And best not to flush tampons—just put in the garbage.

The Cloth Pad

Some find these the most comfortable period items to use. Reusable pads are often made from cotton. They come in different styles and sizes much like a disposable pad but with cloth pattern options for design. A basic cloth pad comes with inserts to make it thicker. When using cloth pads, you need to have a space to wash and let them hang dry.

Most cloth pads have 'wings' that wrap around the crotch of the underwear and snap together on the bottom, to keep the pad in place. Wear it and wash it.

Experiment: The Pad Soak

Repeat 'The Pad Pour' experiment to become familiar with the function of a cloth pad.

Tips & Tricks: "The Rag"

Being on 'the rag' was a slang term used for being on one's period when a piece of cloth was used as a period item. Women have used a piece of cloth through time and still do to this day.

How To Clean Blood Stains

At some point you will end up with blood on your clothes or on your sheets and of course cloth pads if you use them. Hand washing is the best way to clean bloodstains.

What You'll Need

- A small bucket with a lid that you can soak your item, but anything you use will work nicely.
- If you're cleaning underwear or pads, use unscented soap, shampoo or a little bit of laundry soap. As your vagina is a delicate area, it may be sensitive to fragrances. Even if your body doesn't feel too bad, we're not aiming for "too bad," we're aiming for great! And feeling the best possible, is best.
- A place where your pads can hang free to dry. This can be anywhere you're comfortable with.

Tips & Tricks: Cleaning Tips

1. Use cold water only. Using hot water will make a stain harder to take out.
2. Rinse as soon as possible. The longer you leave a stain in, the harder it is to take out and the more stained it becomes. Just rinsing the item in cold water will get rid of some of the stain without even scrubbing.
3. Change water daily if soaking. Still water (water that doesn't move or flow) grows mold.

Hand Washing Technique

- If washing a pad that has inserts, separate the pieces.
- Rinse in cold water or soak for 2-3 hours to prevent staining. Change water daily if it's a hard stain or if you can't take care of the washing the same day.
- Put soap on the stain and rub the two sides of the cloth together, rubbing the stain.
- Rinse and repeat the same steps until the stain is gone.
- Twist the item to get all the water out.
- Hang to dry when possible.

Machine Washing

- Wash with dark colors only in cold water.
- Hang to dry. Don't put in dryer as heat will only make a stain stay if it didn't get out in the wash. It's also hard to tell if the stain is still there until fully dry. Hang to dry and then see if it's gone.

The Sea Sponge

The sea sponge is a natural and reusable tampon alternative that comes from the ocean. It's plant-like, hard when dry and super soft and 'spongy' when damp or wet—hence the name.

Before first use, give it a good soak; rinse in a bucket or a sink filled with water. Swish it around in the water to make sure there aren't any little bits of shell or ocean rocks. Squeeze all the water out with your hand.

Tips & Tricks:
Best Way To Use The Sea Sponge

> The sea sponge absorbs best when just a little bit
> damp and not fully wet.

To Insert

Bunch it up small and compact and then insert with
your fingers. Much like a tampon without an applicator, you have to insert it all the way in so that the ends
to the middle of your fingers disappear into your vagina. If it's too close to the outside of your vagina, it will
be uncomfortable to wear.

Menstrual Cup

The Menstrual Cup is a reusable cup that is inserted
into your vagina to collect period blood. This can be an
option for swimming and recommended for someone
who is comfortable with their vagina and with exploring it. A popular brand is the Diva Cup.

It is folded to insert into your vagina. It creates a suc-
tion cup effect to hug the vagina wall. It also has measurements on the side of the cup so you can see how
much blood comes out.

The cup is taken out, emptied, rinsed and then rein-
serted at least twice in 24 hours. After your period is
finished, it is boiled to sanitize until you use it again. One
cup can last up to 10 years if you take good care of it.

It feels a little odd, like wearing a hat on your head, but quickly becomes second nature.

It's rather big and will push on your hymen. Go as easy as it feels comfortable and give yourself as much time as you need; the slower the better. Using a pad is often naturally a more comfortable choice. A cup is for those more experienced with periods. Use when you've had experience inserting and removing period items from your vagina.

Using A Menstrual Cup

When you feel your vagina is ready to make the move up to a cup, do the following exercises, already explained:

- Meeting Your Cervix and Vagina, *Chapter 3*
- Feeling Your Hymen, *Chapter 6*

Tips & Tricks: Blood Fertilizer

Period blood is a great fertilizer for plants. On your moon, pour it on top of the soil of one of your favorite plants or any plant growing.

Record Your Period Changes

Record changes throughout your entire cycle, not only during your period. Your period is part of a whole system, one part of a cycle and so everything that you experience, every feeling and thought, has to do with one another and connects into your period.

By recording changes and making notes throughout your cycle, you will see the coincidences and things that begin to make sense. The changes will tell you a story.

Even things you may never have thought would have anything to do with one another end up being part of your period story. Looking back on your notes and comments, you may read it like a pattern book with just one look.

]EXERCISE[
Make Your Calendar Key

A period calendar key is a list of symbols that are used to represent things that have to do with your period or things you notice throughout your cycle. They can be emotional, physical and spiritual.

This list of symbols can be used on any calendar or in any diary you wish, as it is a list known only to you.

You can begin by making symbols for some of the suggestions below. Use the descriptions listed as a start to begin making your own. Take away or add anything you like.

Length Of Cycle
First day of period- *An example is using a symbol that will help to remind you like* ℗ *or* ♂
Last day of period

Period Blood
Light flow of blood

Heavy flow of blood
Dark blood
Bright blood

Cervical Fluid Appearance
Thick and creamy white
Yellow
Clear like egg whites

Emotions and Events
This could be anything happening from feeling particularly angry, to sad or confused, brave or strong. You may feel like cleaning everything in your room or not moving a muscle.

7

Nature's Medicine Cabinet

Nature's medicine is carried in plants, the food we eat. It's in the leaves of plants, the fruits and vegetables, the air that green leaves make and the water that grows them.

Plant medicine is the safest, cheapest and quickest way to fix our bodies—and gives us immunization to disease.

Better than pills you find in stores, plants are easiest for your body to use, to consume, to drink. They allow nature to give back to your body what it needs.

Eat dark green leafy vegetables for calcium to strengthen your bones and teeth. For a cold, make tea with lem-

"Plant medicine can be taken as herbal tea, pills or simply eaten as food."

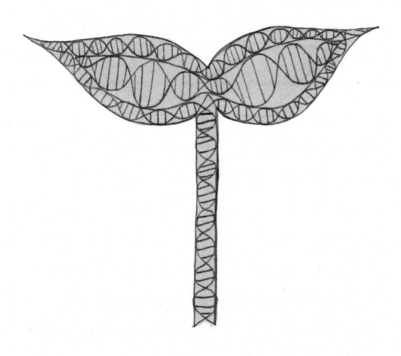

on and ginger. Plants help with everything from acne and hair to infections and the flu.

Plant medicine, especially organic, can help hormones that affect your moon cycle—and everything going on inside of you. Eat organic if it is available.

Today's world is full of food that isn't alive and isn't healing. To see the value your food has, ask yourself these questions: Was it made with love? and Does anyone else know where it came from, including people at the store or your parents? Learn about food that heals your body and gives you nutrition.

Wild Food

Look around to see what food is growing. Plants that grow in the wild make up a huge amount of the life (food) growing on earth. As you pass an apple tree, pick one for you and one for a friend. Eat life.

Growing A Garden, "Plants eat light, eat plants!"

Like our seeds or 'eggs' that are stored in us, information in plants is stored in their seeds, passed down through plant families, gaining strength and wisdom through time.

GMO plants begin as GMO seeds. Many plants in grocery stores grown from genetically modified (GMO) seeds become plants that don't grow seeds in them. No strong plant families. A plant that doesn't make seeds is not good for your reproductive health.

How are seeds grown? With water and light! Put a seed in dirt somewhere where it can get sunlight, like in the windowsill, and water it when it looks like it's getting dry. You can see if it's dry by looking at the top of the soil or by putting your finger in the dirt or 'earth' to see if it's moist or dry below the surface. If it's dry under there, feed it some more water. Growing seeds is the earths magic, learn about nature to get to know the magic of your own body. Start with one seed and grow from there.

For your first women's herb garden, choose seeds that are labeled 'organic,' 'heritage,' 'non-GMO,' and/or 'heirloom.' This means that the seeds being sold have not been altered and are the strongest type of seed that will grow up to be plant medicine and make more seeds.

Learn more about heirloom seeds by reading seed packets, books, asking questions and walking around your local organic market. Ask the names of herbs and plants to find out what they can do for you and your cycle.

Tips and Tricks: Collecting Rose Hips

Rose hips are the fruit of a rose, what is left after the flower gets fertilized and the petals fall off. The rose hip is a fruit, like an apple, and has seeds inside to grow more. A single rose hip the size of a nickel contains 50% more vitamin C than an orange.

Period Medicine

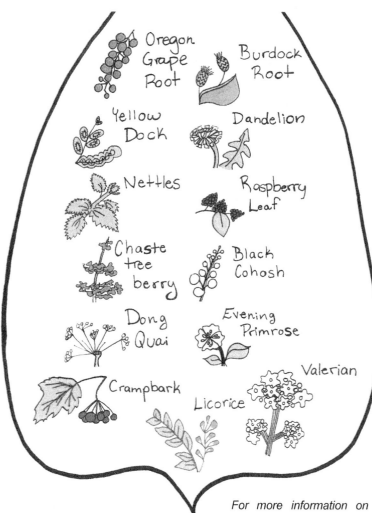

Oregon Grape Root

Burdock Root

Yellow Dock

Dandelion

Nettles

Raspberry Leaf

Chaste tree berry

Black Cohosh

Dong Quai

Evening Primrose

Crampbark

Licorice

Valerian

For more information on these herbs, read 'Wild Medicinal Herbs' at the back of the book.

"Plant medicine is the safest, cheapest and quickest way to fix our bodies— and gives us immunization to disease."

The best time to collect rose hips from rosebushes is in the autumn after the first frost. Watch the rose bushes as they grow and bloom in the spring and summer, as they beautifully unfold their petals. Then watch as their petals fall off and the fruit slowly starts to grow into a red bulb.

Only pick as much as you need. Just collect a small amount from each plant so the plant has enough seeds to grow more roses next year and so other people, animals and birds can have some.

Naturally Healing Period Pains

PMS or Pre-Menstrual Syndrome is the physical and emotional changes that start anywhere between a few days and a week before your period comes.

Some changes in the body include: acne, sensitivity to smell, sensitive breasts or uterine (uterus) cramps. Some changes in your emotions and feelings can include: anger, crying, needing privacy or wanting your room spotless. You name it, women have felt it. Changes are always easier to notice if they are intense.

Tips & Tricks: Womb Love

Drink warm tea, stay in bed and cozy up with warm blankets around you to keep warm. Focus on the area you're feeling pain in and love it until the pain goes away. Thinking directly about the area in pain with love helps for some reason. Try it.

Period cramps, aches and pains are sometimes felt from mild to strong during your period time. Cramps during your period are the feeling of your uterus, which is a muscle, using its strength to squeeze itself and get the blood to flow out.

But just because you get a period, doesn't mean it has to hurt. For some women period time is like the rest of the month, but a time when they turn inward to look at their thoughts and pay more attention to how they feel. Some women also don't notice the effects of PMS; so don't expect anything, just watch and feel.

If you experience bad cramps, you'll want nothing better than to comfort yourself and keep yourself warm if you're feeling cold. Roll yourself up in some comfy blankets or press a hot water bottle to your womb, on top of your uterus area.

Physically connect with the earth while you're on your period. Jump into a lake, take off your shoes and walk on the bare ground (not cement), stand on a rock, lay or roll on the grass, or hug a tree.

The earth will heal you and she needs you to heal her.

"Nature's medicine is carried in plants."

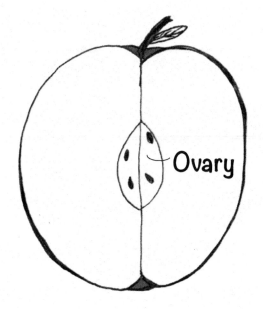

Ovary

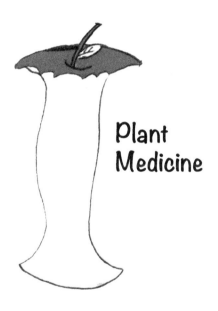

Plant
Medicine

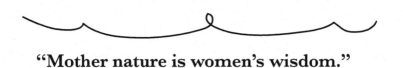

"Mother nature _is_ women's wisdom."

The earth is mother to us all, and when you need healing, go straight to her. To the oceans and the lakes, the trees and the dirt, the plants that grow as medicine straight from the earth. Mother nature is women's wisdom.

'Earthing' or 'grounding' is better than a painkiller. This will help with PMS, period pain and your over-all health, like plant medicine that helps all of you, because you are also a part of nature. These things will also prevent pain and big emotions from coming around your next cycle.

Reduce the amount of junk food you eat while on your moon time and take your plant medicine. Notice how much a can of pop or handful of candy will increase your mood swings and how you get irritated by people, have more acne or become more sensitive. If you feel like chocolate, consider alternatives that have less sugar and more magnesium (which is what you crave in the chocolate) like: kale, dark leafy greens or quinoa.

Do some fun exercise on the days you don't feel like curling up. Exercise helps calm PMS, period cramps, aches and pains.

You will be surprised to know your body reacts to your thoughts about it. Pay attention to what you think about yourself and your body. Try thinking about how strong you are and what a great woman you are, how beautiful your period is happening inside you and how amazing it is that a baby can grow inside of your uterus.

Supplements

Tea and herbal supplements are dried and crushed herbs. Crushed, the same way a leaf breaks up in your hand after it dries. Herbs can then be put into pill form after they are crushed so you can swallow it, or soak it in a tea bag form, so that you can drink it. Herbs are also eaten fresh.

Supplements are another way to eat herbs and plant medicine when you don't have fresh plants and herbs around. Look in your local health food store for supplements or teas with magnesium and iron, two things that support your reproductive system. Look for teas that say 'women's time' or 'moon time tea.' Drink teas heavy with iron, like nettle, red raspberry leaf, dandelion and yellow dock.

Taking Pain Pills For Symptoms

The 'symptoms' of PMS can be strong emotions and physical pain—like cramps.

Period pain pills like Advil and Midol make you feel

symptoms less. Symptoms are a sign of sickness, but not the cause of the sickness. Like coughing when you have a cold, the cough is the 'symptom' and the cold virus is the 'cause.'

The pain pill tricks your body into thinking nothing is wrong, but in fact, it just hides the symptoms from you. The cause of your period cramps are still there.

Period pills make you feel your emotions and physical pain less, which can be great if you are experiencing terrible cramps and headaches.

Symptoms can only be cured for a short time though because the origin of the pain isn't helped, and so, the pain comes back again and again, period after period.

If you take a pill, period after period, it's hard to know what you're body is telling you when you're yelling at it to stop! How will you know what is happening in your body if you can't feel it happening? Pills take away lots of little feelings too, not only the pain. This makes it hard to 'listen' to your body and learn how to take care of it.

Remember that pain is a signal that something must be changed or helped. To remedy the cause of period pains, we must remember to use the earth; she is our mother and has the answers we need.

There can be situations that healthy remedies can't cure fast enough. If period pain and problems continue, seek out a health care provider.

How Your Mother Got Pregnant

Sperm are the sacred seeds carried in men that contain information to make life.

They are the partner to your egg, the other half of what is needed to make a baby. Together, they make a whole.

The two testes or 'balls,' which are just underneath and to the sides of the penis, are where the sperm is made, much like the two ovaries found in a woman.

We're more alike than we are different. All these parts are just placed differently. We both have a urethra and two main areas on either side for the seeds to be car-

"There is no 'one way' to make love with another person."

ried. The penis and vagina are quite similar also: one goes outward outside the body and one inward inside the body. Together they fit.

The long part (length) of the penis is called the shaft and the top is called the head. Its head looks like a hat and is very sensitive with many nerve endings, much like your clitoris.

The tube called the urethra that goes through the middle of the shaft is used for sperm and pee to come out of one hole for both. The urethra leads to the bladder where pee is held.

Sperm are delicate. They are much tinier than your eggs and have little tails to swim. They are safely carried out of the body in liquid called semen to meet the egg.

This liquid makes it possible for the sperm to be inside a man's body and then go outside and into a woman's. The semen travels through the shaft of the penis and out through the tip of the head. When the semen comes out this is called ejaculation or 'coming.'

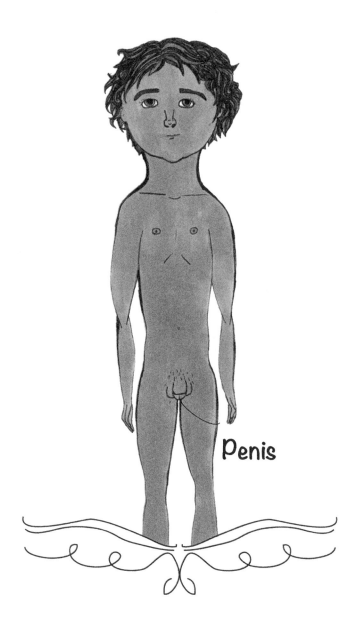

Penis

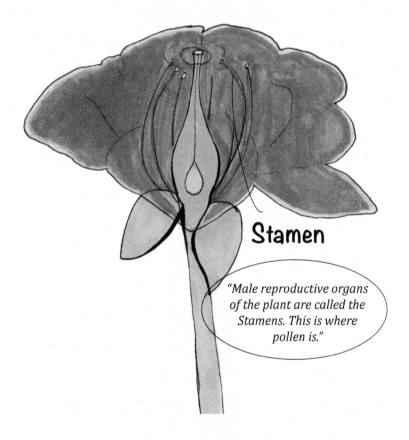

Stamen

"Male reproductive organs of the plant are called the Stamens. This is where pollen is."

If semen gets inside the vagina, sperm will swim in search of an egg, through the cervix, into the uterus and fallopian tubes. They don't know where the egg is, only that they have to find it.

One ejaculation can have anywhere from 14 million to 1 billion sperm. It only takes one sperm to fertilize an egg.

Sperm will survive for up to a week inside your uterus and fallopian tubes in search of an egg. When and if sperm find your egg, they will nuzzle it to try and get in. If and when the egg wall opens up to allow a sperm to enter, conception has occurred.

After this, the fertilized egg will travel to the period lining inside your uterus and plant itself there, in the softest place with just the right nutrients.

The specific egg and specific sperm make a new being. Together, they will grow into a fetus, and if it continues to grow, it will be born into a baby.

Sex

People have sex for pleasure and with different types of people: people they are married to, people who are the same gender (women with women or men with men), people they are dating or just getting to know and even with friends.

Feelings come first. We show them through talking, walking, kissing, handholding and touching. These

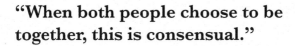

"When both people choose to be together, this is consensual."

things allow you to see how you feel with the other person. Your feelings let you know if you can trust someone and let them in. When you trust a partner, you feel it; your body opens up. Many women feel sex is best if they wait until they find a sexual partner they trust. Trust is part of love, and sex is often better when you love and are loved.

When both people choose to be together, this is consensual. Explore the feeling of pleasure together. Discover how you like to be touched and how you like to touch someone else. There is no one way to make love or have sex with another person; the ways are as unique as you are.

Usually people start out by touching each other. Getting close: sitting beside each other on a couch, looking into each others eyes to see how you're feeling: touching someone's arm, waist or leg: having a kiss and touching their face. As the urge to explore and see what they look like naked comes, more clothes are taken off or pushed aside to see their belly, their legs, their chest, to feel their bare skin with your hands or against your body.

The more that touching happens, desire and energy increase in the body. Blood rushes to the genitals, and the vagina and penis get warmer, larger and moister.

Before the excitement of sex, the penis is soft like a droopy tongue, and as he gets excited blood rushes in to fill it, making it hard and firm like when you stick your tongue straight out to touch something. This is called an erection. When a penis is firm and points outward it is able to enter a vagina.

The vagina also changes in her own way. Blood enters the vaginal walls and can make the vagina expand up to twice its size. The vagina becomes slippery and wet with fluid. This is lubrication; a little will also come out of the head of the penis. Anticipating sex, your body will create this lubrication, getting ready as you have become aroused or 'turned on.'

Like when your mouth waters at the sight of your favorite meal, saliva comes in to prepare itself for the meal. Your vagina does the same in preparation for sex. Lubrication makes everything feel softer and more sensitive. It makes it more comfortable to insert a finger or a penis during sex.

Touching each other's genitals is part of the process. This is called 'mutual masturbation' and can be very intimate and part of foreplay (a sexual act before sex) or a sexually intimate act all by itself. It's how you get to know what it feels like to touch and be touched.

You come to know what you like by being in sexual situations. You decide what you like based on your experiences, including the time you spend by yourself, touching yourself, slowly and gently to unfold your feelings. Remembering that the folds on your vulva are like the petals of a flower, and a flower takes time to open. A flower can't be forced or hurried, the same as your body and your feelings can't be hurried.

Touching yourself is sometimes called 'masturbation,' but this word doesn't describe the beautiful experience that you can have, the gentleness and beauty when you give yourself affection.

If you want the person you're with to know how you would like to be touched, it's easiest to guide them if they're watching you. You can also take their hands and show them.

Tips & Tricks: Honesty & Eye Contact

To create a feeling of security between both of you, look at the person you're with and show them how to look at you. If they see your eyes, your smile, your look of truth and freedom they seek, they'll be even happier to see you.

When the time comes that you want to prepare yourself to have penetration sex, make it safe sex. Read more about using protection and birth control options in 'Birth Control: The Choice of Having Children.'

"To create a feeling of security, look at the person you're with and show them how to look at you."

"You find out how you like to be touched based on your experiences, including the time you spend by yourself, touching yourself, slowly and gently to unfold your feelings."

How do you know if you're ready? You body feels open, and you feel love and trust. You feel 'yes.'

Being **heterosexual** doesn't mean you have to have penetration sex; it can simply and happily be an exploration of finding pleasure with someone else. It can be the excited happy feeling of sharing a kiss, holding hands or being comfortable enough with someone to look into their eyes.

To make a baby, though, takes penetration sex. Usually starting with lots of touching. As the loving and excited touching increases so does the natural lubrication that helps the penis enter the vagina more easily and comfortably for the woman. How the penis enters and moves around are best decided by how the woman feels.

During sex, the friction of the skin of the penis gliding in and out of the vagina, or even being rubbed by a

"Making love is happily an exploration of pleasure with someone else."

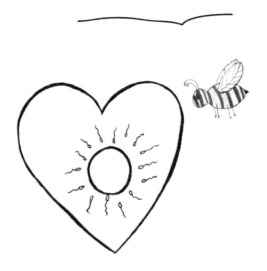

hand, will make male excitement come to a peak. This can sometimes happen with no touch at all, just the feeling of excitement peaking. At this moment there is a burst or 'orgasm' and the man ejaculates semen, which carries sperm, the male's sacred seeds.

These are the basics of having sex for 'how to make a baby.' This does not cover all the details of how women experience pleasure. So keep exploring your beautiful interesting self to see how you unfold.

9

Birth Control: The Choice Of Having Children

Birth control is the right to prevent pregnancy.

By having a period, your body is saying 'yes' to pregnancy every month. If you choose to become pregnant, you simply do not prevent pregnancy.

You will most likely become pregnant if you have sex and don't use some method of birth control. If you choose not to choose—by not using birth control—you're still choosing. You're choosing to become pregnant.

The invention of birth control has given women the opportunity to continue having sex for fun and pleasure

"By simply having a period, your body is saying 'yes' to pregnancy every month."

without getting pregnant.

Birth control, such as the pill and condoms, are a substitute for having intimate knowledge about your female body and your cycle. With more knowledge about your cycle, you are able to practice natural methods of birth control.

Making a decision to get pregnant or to prevent pregnancy is important to make before even using birth control. Take time out with yourself. Know your heart, the blood pumping through it and how it feels. Feel the choice in your body, and then act on it.

If YOUR choice is not to become pregnant, avoid sexual intercourse or use birth control or condoms. The possibilities to explore sensuality can be a lot more fun than only having sex.

Knowing your feelings comes first, and then acting on them second. By USING birth control, you are acting on your choice to prevent pregnancy.

You are the one to take responsibility for your body.

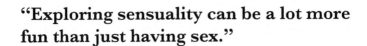

"Exploring sensuality can be a lot more fun than just having sex."

You are the oven, or incubator, used to grow an entire life inside you. Your say is the most important and your period is a reminder of the present you have, to become pregnant, if you choose.

You have full choice and control over your body—no exceptions. The period at the end of the sentence is a good reminder that you have the last say over your body, period. Go with your gut.

You have more choices than you can count.

You can choose to have sex, not have sex, use protection, not use protection, just be sexual but with no penetration, kiss a lot, date girls, and explore all the sensual feelings your body has to offer you.

How To Become Pregnant

To become pregnant, have sex without using condoms or birth control. Your body's natural state is to try and become pregnant.

The easiest time for you to become pregnant is during

Ovulation. To know when you're ovulating, check your cervical fluid. Slippery, egg-white clear, cervical fluid helps sperm to travel up into your fallopian tubes in search of a ripe egg. This is the time in your cycle when your vagina feels best and the time in your cycle when you feel most sexual.

Your basal body temperature experiment will also come in handy when appreciating how to become pregnant (see 'Chapter 4, The Reproductive Cycle'). When your temperature has increased, you are a few days away from ovulating and can begin having unprotected sex.

Other ways of becoming pregnant that don't include having sex are called **reproductive technology**. For example, going to sperm banks where you can have donated sperm inserted into your body.

There are also many ways of becoming a mother that don't include sex or men. There is adopting or having a surrogate mother, which is another woman who carries your egg fertilized by a sperm inside her until it grows into a baby, then she gives birth for you.

How To Not Get Pregnant

Don't have sex, or choose to use birth control if you don't want a pregnancy. Many forms of birth control are available if you are interested in using one. The Pill, as explained below, is only one commonly used option. Speak to a health care provider or check out a 'teen clinic' if you don't have a doctor or if you want more anonymity.

The Pill

The Pill created a revolution for women's birth control choices when women were having an average of 4-16 babies in their lifetime.

The Birth Control Pill is a small pill you take every day that changes your natural chemistry—your hormones, the rhythm of your emotions and moods.

The Pill makes lovemaking a possibility without the high potential of pregnancy and has many side effects. The side effects depend on your health, the person taking the birth control and the type of pill. When considering whether to take the pill, talk to a health care provider to understand the side effects of each type of pill.

Used properly, the pill is effective 91% of the time. You need to take it daily. It does not protect you from getting STIs (Sexually Transmitted Infections).

Condoms

Condoms are worn over top of the penis to prevent semen from going into the vagina. Condoms are usually made of latex, but many new types of condoms are made out of other materials. A condom holds and catches the semen in the tip when used properly.

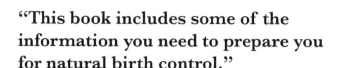

"This book includes some of the information you need to prepare you for natural birth control."

Condoms not only prevent pregnancy but also many STIs. Not only do they prevent sperm from exiting the condom but they also reduce skin to skin touching and can stop fluid from being exchanged. Use condoms to protect yourself from fear of pregnancy and disease. If you are unsure of what you want, use a condom.

Used properly, condoms are effective 98% of the time. Condoms protect you from getting STIs (Sexually Transmitted Infections) and prevent pregnancy.

Natural Birth Control Methods

Many types of natural birth control options will require some knowledge of your body and cycle—knowledge that you will gain over time. This book includes some of the information you need to prepare you for natural birth control: following your period on the calendar, noticing changes in cervical fluid and recording your basal body temperature.

Using the wetness of your vagina to determine what

"It is important to prevent pregnancy if it's not what you want."

time of your cycle you're in. When there's blood, you're on your period. Just before your period comes, the stuff on your underwear is usually a little thicker. After your period, there isn't much stuff on your underwear.

Natural birth control methods are like knowing what season it is and when to plant seeds. Most likely if you plant seeds in the spring when the sun comes out, your seeds will grow in the garden; if you plant seeds in the winter, nothing will happen.

If you have sex during a certain time in your cycle, you're less likely to get pregnant than if you have sex in a different time.

If you are going to wait to have sex until you know your body and cycle intimately, then spend some time researching natural birth control methods. If you are going to have sex sooner, then you may want to use a condom and some kind of birth control when starting out. Our bodies take years to understand, and the use of natural methods may take some time.

Ultimately you want to get to know yourself—you're

very interesting! If you use the birth control pill, the effects of the pill will make it harder to tell exactly what's going on in your body because it changes the body's natural environment. That's just something to keep in mind. Understanding your body is important to be able to understand how to care for it.

Abortion

Abortion is a matter of the heart. A procedure that removes a fetus from inside a uterus or 'womb.'

The heart and womb are both places of deep feeling inside a woman, which can fill with love or hurt if not honored.

Honoring your heart is done by listening to it and making decisions with it that affect your body and your life. Feelings are taken to heart.

Just to speak of abortion is a call to action. Meaning that just to know what abortion is and that it is an option should call you to consider your choices. Most importantly you need to think about how to prevent pregnancy if it isn't what you want.

If the choice to prevent pregnancy before having sex isn't made and you become pregnant, you are still left with a choice to make, to either have a baby or an abortion, neither of which may have been your first choice. Choice can only be delayed, not avoided.

When the decision hasn't been made either way, the result is indifference. A solid choice must be made to take pride in your journey of life and as a woman with choices. If you make the decision to have an abortion based on what other people want—a boyfriend, parent or friend—then you will have to live with your decision of not making your own choice.

When a decision is made to have an abortion, and it goes against what is felt in a woman's heart, then deep hurt may be felt. In this case one of the many feelings left with a woman after an abortion may be the feeling that she didn't make her choice from the deepest place within her.

There are many reasons why women have abortions other than not using birth control. Often, the reasons are that either birth control didn't work or sex was forced or without **consent**.

Use your feelings as a guiding light. Consider your options to make your choices of course, to take into account what you want the most, and to not be overly swayed by others' definitions of what the right choice is for you. Trust yourself.

Morning After Pill or Emergency Pill

Often known as Plan B, this is a low dose of hormone that can interfere with a pregnancy before it starts.

Taken within 5 days of unprotected sex, it is usually avail-

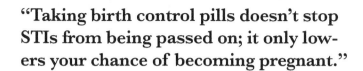

"Taking birth control pills doesn't stop STIs from being passed on; it only lowers your chance of becoming pregnant."

able in drug stores, no prescription needed depending on where you live.

STIs (Sexually Transmitted Infections)

STIs are also known as **STDs** but are the same thing. One is 'Sexually Transmitted Infection' and the other is 'Sexually Transmitted Disease.'

Numerous types of STIs are passed on mainly from unprotected sex. They can be found in anyone with or without you knowing. Using protection is as much for preventing you from getting an STI as it is for preventing you from getting pregnant.

There are tests both women and men can take to tell if they have an STI.

When or before, you start to have sex with someone, it's best to both be tested if you've been sexually active before. Often people don't know they have an infection.

Tips & Tricks:
Having Power at the Doctor's Office

As part of a **PAP** test, a speculum is inserted into your vagina and opened a little to see your cervix. If it makes you more comfortable to insert it yourself, just ask the doctor beforehand. Ask questions so you can understand what is happening and why. There is no 'dumb' question; everything you want to know is worth asking. You can also write down questions you have before you go into your appointment. Just because doctors know more, doesn't mean they make decisions for you; it means you have someone you can ask questions.

The wise wearer of a condom can feel confident that they are helping to protect themselves from STIs. If a person you want to have sex with doesn't want to use a condom, it's better to just not have sex. You can take the blame if they get upset, or you can be the confident teacher in this situation instead of taking on an infection. Use your influence and make yourself be heard.

STIs can be found in anyone, even people you trust. Make use of protection that's available. Get tested, have him wear a condom and use birth control if you have chosen to prevent a pregnancy from happening.

10

Birth

Pregnancy

A fetus (growing baby not born yet) will grow and develop in your uterus for approximately nine months, often shorter or longer but always in its own time.

Your uterus will stretch to make room for a growing fetus. Inside your uterus, the fetus will transform into a whole new person, the unfolding of a seed within you.

Your body will provide shelter and nourishment for a growing fetus. Growing in a sac full of liquid or 'amniotic fluid,' it will sway and be protected until the time of birth. All of the nutrients that a fetus needs go

"Contractions are when your uterus starts contracting or 'squeezing' and your cervix opens. It's just like period cramps but more intense."

through an umbilical cord that connects the placenta, a special organ. Nutrients go straight into the baby's blood stream, not through the mouth.

The belly button you have is the remainder of the cord that was cut, connecting you and the placenta, after you came out of your mother's womb.

While pregnant, the energy of a mother is used to create life. During pregnancy your body will completely transform to make room for a fetus and will be in need of nutritious food to care for itself as it cares for a fetus.

Birth

The birth process is where many things happen together, like in your cycle. Labor is the time of the birthing process before actual birth when the baby comes out. A woman can be in labor from anywhere between a few hours to a few days.

Part of the birth process is that your water breaks,

which means the amniotic sac starts leaking or breaks to let the water out. The amniotic fluid or 'water' comes out of your vagina first, and some comes out with the baby as lubrication.

The hole in the middle of your cervix dilates or opens. This part of the birth process starts slow and small at one centimeter in diameter and opens up to 10 centimeters with contractions to allow for the baby to pass through. Contractions are when your uterus starts contracting or 'squeezing' and your cervix opens. It's just like period cramps but more intense because the uterus is now much bigger and so is the weight of everything inside the amniotic sac.

The uterus, being a muscle, squeezes and tightens in contractions. Contractions start lightly and small with a long period of time between them. As time moves on, contractions come more frequent and become more painful. When there isn't any more time in between contractions, birth is taking place; the baby is about to come out. The body is pressing down to help it make its way out.

The contractions give the baby small steps of slowly coming down the birth canal until it's all the way out.

There is a crossing from an underwater world into a new air-filled world. As the baby crosses the threshold through the vagina, its lungs get a little squeeze so when it comes out, it takes its first breath.

"Breast milk is the most nutritious food for a human baby."

Breast Milk: A Magic Elixir

Your breast milk is made in your **milk sacs** or glands after the baby is born. All women with breasts can make milk—it doesn't matter if the breasts are small or large.

Breast milk is triggered to start when the baby comes out as your body knows what is happening inside you. The baby sucking at a nipple also triggers the milk to come out.

The first milk that comes out is clear and the most nutritious. As the feeding continues, the milk turns white.

Breast milk is the most nutritious food for a human baby. A mother's body produces breast milk especially for the needs of the baby. Women's bodies can actually tell what babies need and makes it especially for them.

As the baby's health needs change, so does the milk. Although you wouldn't be able to tell with your eyes, it's magic at work.

Babies may also drink formula out of a bottle as a substitute instead of breast milk.

Birthing Spirits

Your spirit is your spark, the you that shines through. Much like your nature, it's the way you are that is different from everyone else.

Birthing spirits is like destiny, a completely new body, and spirit to fill a new body.

With birth is the right to your voice. From your first cry as a baby announcing your arrival, using your sound.

Your spirit is heard in your words, your voice, your movements, your dreams, your ambitions, your art, your love. Holding the truth of you high for you to see through your emotions, your plans, your forgiveness and your tales.

Spirit is contained in a seed.

Being born is a journey to yourself, to sing your true song, and can only be found in a place known to you. It's your secret pleasure to find, to express, to experience yourself.

The moon is your mirror, your friend. She puts the light on in the night and shows you to look with your heart and not with your eyes, to use your senses as your guide and look within for the answers. In you is where you find your song, your sound of truth.

Birth is a rite of passage, a crossing over into a new way of life. A right to one's own name. Claim it, say it like you chose it.

This new passage into womanhood is your most recent rite.

Your first period is a new time of claiming yourself and that which is in you. Using this voice, your voice, to express how you feel, to make choices that no one else can make for you, making your voice heard. Let your true voice be heard over the crowd. Seeing what you like in the world, feeling it and unlocking your heart to shine and show your true colors.

Becoming your own woman, by right.

Author's Note

This book was a journey into womanhood for me just as much as it was for my daughter. As a woman with a deep sense of knowing, I still had so much to learn.

Period books and teachers always made me feel like I was missing something, like I was supposed to have this mysterious base of knowledge all people agreed on.

They skipped to the science of periods before considering how I felt about the idea of period blood—the gushy red stuff that I had mixed emotions about. My ball of feelings about blood was a mix: everything I'd seen in T.V. programs, social shame, death and hospitals.

Like we were all comfortable enough around sex and reproductive anatomy that we could have a class on the technical aspects before addressing our discomfort. These undiscovered feelings were the doors, the gatekeepers, that let information in and out. Without talking about our feelings, we were playing it cool, acting like we were comfortable.

I started writing The Moon In You when I was 29 years old. What started as a 16-page hand-drawn pamphlet became a soul life learning to fill the missing piece. At the time I began with my daughter. We were living in a friend's small spare room, and from the first draft to the last, Leighyah and I moved five times, gave up our belongings three times and opened up to a new way of living: creatively. As we spent less time focusing on money (how we spent it and earned it), we were able to focus on the natural world, healing properties of plants, subtleties of nature and, of course, ourselves.

Our first big move that propelled our journey took us from Toronto to the West Coast. We landed on Salt Spring Island and took in all the island had to offer: wild plant life, a supportive community, nurturing women, and time to talk and be. A small place without the distractions of marketing and advertising to divert our attention.

We started growing food together, our first garden. Something harder to do in the city with little money and no land. I deepened, my daughter deepened, and we deepened together.

I used my newly found time to research female reproductive anatomy and plant reproduction to understand women as being a part of nature, not 'apart.' I learned about the cycle of an egg AND the moon. To understand the unfolding from puberty to maturity, I watched a bud slowly unfold into a full blooming flower. I further developed my intuition by spending many hours meditating on my womb, sending light in and listening to the subtleties of my body through its cycle. I showed my period love.

On my way to becoming a period-loving woman, I learned even more important things: how to feel my feelings, identify my feelings, feel what was my heart feeling, use my voice and speak up and follow my intuition. I learned to not be a stranger in my own skin.

I'm so thankful we ended up taking this adventure and living on this small island so we could give you a piece of it in this book. It was a safe haven for a delicate person like myself to birth this baby of a book. Its kind people and space cradled me into letting go instead of shocking me into keeping shut.

An Epilogue for Mother's Uniting

Now that the book has ended, answer me this: how did you like it? And do you like yourself better after reading it? This period book isn't just a book; it's a look into the lives of girls and women that matter. It is an opportunity to heal and see how far we've come. A time to unearth our radiance, energy and light.

For a long time now women have been taken from. But now, in numbers, it's time for us to take it to the streets. Us, that is.

Wearing flowers behind our ears, we will all line up with our children our sisters and apologize for nothing, to take back our human rights as females. As we let go of the past, we will walk forward, a global family of women under one roof—the sky.

And one more thing we ask as we move together, a clan with a plan—who are we? Mothers? Leaders? Freedom seekers? We do many jobs, go by many names, yet no one applauds our many tasks. No one takes us seriously unless we accept payment as recognition for our efforts. In negotiating this price of freedom, we must first feel worthy enough to hear our own inner voice. To use it, because knowledge must have a voice.

Here, we free each other from the thousands of years of silence. We are becoming and raising a new era of up-spoken women, who bleed through and who yearn to hear the tone of their truth so deeply that it resonates in their bones.

Today is the day to wave our flag of forgiveness on earth, because it is not until we openly forgive that the peace treaty is signed. And under one roof we will fall to our knees. Under the flag of peace, open our arms and explode with love, with hugs, for our sisters and brothers and children and mothers. Our grandmothers, now gone and passed away will clap for the progress we have made together, as one. And we go into the future, the now, we will promise ourselves all the roses our blessed hearts can take, all the love we can muster and all the cake we can eat because look what's inside of us! Great love just waiting to be unbound, waiting to burst out. Waiting to love so violently that there will never be room for people to be violent ever again.

Your heart is a force to be reckoned with—for its magnitude, its heat, its might! Your age has little to do with the power of your heart. You are timeless, your power is timeless, and your power makes you beautiful, in all your ages.

Dictionary

Abortion- the termination of a pregnancy before the fetus is able to survive on its own outside of the womb, usually done in the first 14 weeks.

Alternative healing methods (alternative medicine)- healing that isn't based solely in evidence and science, although it can be a science (i.e., Naturopath, Osteopath, Herbalist, Chinese Medicine, Ayurvedic Medicine).

Anus- the entrance to your rectum from which poo comes out.

Areola- the colored circle area around the nipple.

Basal body temperature- the lowest body temperature you have in 24 hours.

Birth control- controlling the outcome of your fertility, often referring to the usage of hormonal birth control that prevents you from becoming pregnant by changing your natural chemistry and hormones.

Breast buds- as your breasts start to grow during puberty, they form a hard lump underneath your nipples.

Cervical fluid- a fluid made by the cervix that changes texture throughout the reproductive cycle, from thin and clear like egg whites to white or yellowish and chunky like yoghurt.

Cervix- a mini donut-shaped passage between your uterus and vagina with a small hole in the center.

Circumcised (also see Uncircumcised)- When a fold of skin that covers the penis head is cut off, usually as a baby. The penis, like the vagina, has skin that folds over the delicate opening, like the Labia Majora that covers the entrance to the vagina. It is this covering that is cut off.

The Female Reproductive System

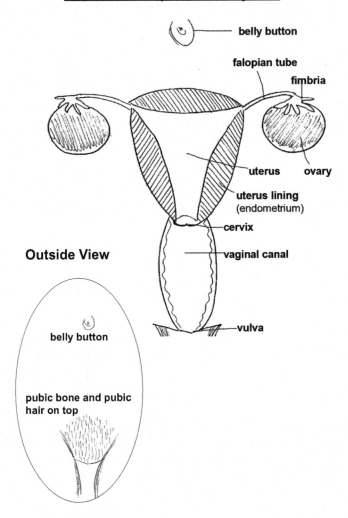

belly button

falopian tube

fimbria

uterus   ovary

uterus lining
(endometrium)

cervix

Outside View

vaginal canal

vulva

belly button

pubic bone and pubic
hair on top

Clitoris- A very small pea-sized part of the genitalia that is highly sensitive and made for pleasure. Appears small but the larger part of it is inside the body. Called a 'clit' for short.

Consent- an agreement or permission to do or allow something. In particular for the subject of this book, consent to touch, have sexual or intimate contact with someone else. Both people must consent.

Egg- women's sex cell containing information to make life, one half to what is needed to make a baby. Actual name is 'ova.'

Ejaculation- when semen squirts out through the tip of the penis as the result of orgasm.

Endometrium- The uterus lining that thickens and sheds.

Erection- when blood fills the penis to make it firm, making the penis lift up, stick out and become larger.

Fallopian tubes- the tubes on either side of the uterus connecting ovaries to uterus through which the egg takes its journey.

Fertilization (conception)- when the sperm enters the egg to fertilize it and together the information in both the egg and the sperm come together and make the beginnings of a baby.

Fimbria- the little tentacles or hands at the end of the fallopian tube that wait to catch a matured egg.

Foreplay- Sexual activity that isn't penetration sex, usually happening before sex to build energy and excitement.

Heterosexual- when you are sexually attracted to people of the opposite sex. If someone were attracted to both genders, they would be bisexual.

Hormones- chemical messages that influence your body to mature and make changes.

Hymen- a thin layer of skin that surrounds or partially covers your vagina. Can be many different shapes and thicknesses.

Intuition- The feelings that you can't explain that help guide you in your life.

Labia majora (outer vulva lips)- the lips on the outside of the external genitalia that can be any shape from flowery and frilly to smooth and straight.

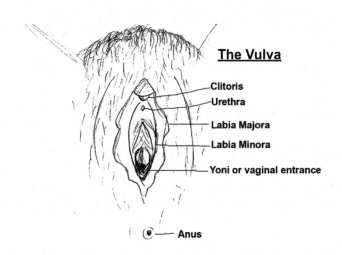

The Vulva

- Clitoris
- Urethra
- Labia Majora
- Labia Minora
- Yoni or vaginal entrance
- Anus

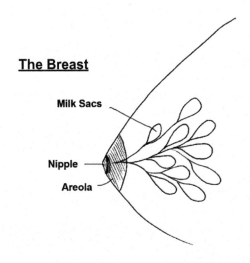

The Breast

- Milk Sacs
- Nipple
- Areola

Labia minora (small vulva lips)- part of the external genitalia that is smooth, sensitive and hairless located on the inside of the Labia Majora.

Milk sacs (mammary glands)- the sacs that grow in your breast and fill with milk during pregnancy and after birth.

Mound of venus (pubic bone)- the bump of flesh and bone underneath your pubic hair.

Nipple- the point or little bump at the tip of your breasts, may also be inverted (turned inward).

Organic- food that isn't sprayed with chemicals.

Orgasm- the height of pleasurable energy when muscle and cardiovascular energy peak, when energy builds so much that your body can't contain it, and it overflows.

Ovary- an organ the size of a shelled walnut where all of your non-matured eggs are kept and mature.

Ovulation- a mature egg or 'ovum' exploding out of an ovary.

PAP Smear- a test for women that collects samples from your vagina and cervix to test for STIs and cervical cancer.

Penetration sex- when a penis enters a vagina or anus.

Period, Menstruation, Moon time- 1) When blood comes out through your vagina about once a month for a few days to a week, 2) When your uterus lining sheds at the end of your cycle and comes out through your vagina, 3) The result of an unfertilized egg.

PMS (Pre Menstrual Syndrome)- intense or usually noticeable feelings or behavior a few days up to a week before your period begins from hormonal changes.

Puberty- Your body maturing, going through physical changes, to the point when you have your period (for girls) and can make children.

Pubic hair- hair covering your mound of venus and vulva.

Reproductive technology- technology that helps you become pregnant or not pregnant, such as in vitro fertilization, artificial insemination or contraception.

Scrotum- skin covering the testes or 'balls.'

Semen- the liquid that comes out of the tip of the penis when he has an orgasm. Also known as 'cum.'

The Penis

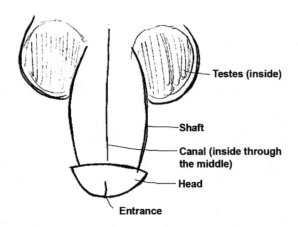

Testes (inside)

Shaft

Canal (inside through the middle)

Head

Entrance

Shaft- the long section of the penis that turns from soft to hard when filled with blood.

Sperm- man's sex cell containing information to make life, one half to what is needed to make a baby.

STDs (Sexually Transmitted Disease)- the same as STIs.

STIs (Sexually Transmitted Infections)- an infection that is passed or spread through sexual activity, not only through penetration sex but also through fluids exchanging and skin touching.

Testes (testicles)- balls inside the scrotum where sperm is produced.

The Morning After Pill- hormone pills taken within 5 days of unprotected sex to prevent pregnancy.

The Pill- a hormone pill taken daily which alters your cycle and prevents pregnancy.

'The seed'- egg or sperm containing genetic information passed down through generations.

Uncircumcised (also see Circumcised)- When the fold of skin that covers the top of the penis head is not cut off, it is left as is.

Urethra- the tube that leads to your bladder which pee comes out of.

Uterus (womb or baby room)- a muscle where a baby would grow if you were pregnant and where period blood comes from.

Vagina- the canal that leads from the vagina opening to the cervix and then to the uterus.

Vulva- your external genitalia between your mound of venus and anus.

Yoni (vaginal entrance)- entrance to the divine.

Wild Medicinal Herbs

Materia Medica for Every Woman's Cycle

Use this Materia Medica to enrich your knowledge of women's herbs. Women's medicine is earth medicine.

For thousands of years women have worked with the earth, drank its water, ate its food, healed with its plants. It's only our most recent history that our knowledge of herbs has been removed and replaced with pharmaceuticals, without knowing where medicine comes from. Healing knowledge and trust has been put into doctors and pills, and it is time to remember healing knowledge. Begin with learning the names of herbs, like 'dong quai.' Learn 'plant talk' by learning how people speak about plants (i.e., the 'properties' a plant has) and by listening to your intuition. Learn about the qualities of each herb and their ability to heal. Humans need to better recognize and know their plant friends and allies.

Caution/Awareness: Taking herbs is not a game; they are powerful medicine. Never put anything in your mouth that you are not sure how to use. This Materia Medica is intended as guidance to learn about the abilities of plants as medicine. For instruction of what to take and how much, make an appointment with a trained herbalist.

Drug interactions: Consult with an herbalist before taking herbs for healing, especially if you are taking medication, even if that medication is only Advil. Herbs are powerful medicine; they can be sedatives, good for the nerves, can induce labor or make you fertile. It is unsafe to take particular herbs in conjunction with pharmaceutical drugs.

List of Herbs

Black Cohosh
Burdock
Chaste Tree
Cramp Bark
Dandelion
Dong Quai
Evening Primrose
Licorice
Nettles
Oregon Grape Root
Raspberry Leaf
Valerian

 Black Cohosh

Common Name: Black Cohosh
Latin Name: Cimicifuga racemosa
Plant family: Ranunculaceae
Common parts used: rhizome and root
Actions: analgesic, anti-inflammatory, antispasmodic, hypo-tensive, nervine
Energetics: cooling, drying

Description: Known as a 'woman's herb.' This perennial plant blooms a long cluster of white flowers and grows up to 10 inches high.

Uses (common and uncommon): Used to regulate female

imbalances. A powerful uterine tonic that relieves menstrual pain and regulates hormones during puberty, a woman's cycle and menopause. A uterine stimulant, and relaxant, used to bring on delayed menstruation or stimulate labor.

As an anti-inflammatory, it is good for arthritis, muscular and neurological pain. A nerve and muscle relaxant. It has been used for headaches, aches & pains, muscle spasms, rheumatism and neuralgia.

Safety Issues and Precautions: Non-toxic. Avoid using during pregnancy, except the last month of pregnancy when it can then be used to stimulate labor.

Planting/Growing: Grows plentifully in rich woodland soil.

Harvesting: When the leaves of a mature plant turn yellow around the edges, it's time to collect the roots. As with the collection of all herbal roots, autumn time is best. It's when the flowers and top of the plant fade, and the energy of the plant goes down into the roots.

*At-risk plant. Because black cohosh is an at-risk plant, be sure to break a small piece of the root off when harvesting and sew back into the soil so it may grow another plant in its place.

Menstruation notation: Balances hormones. Helps with painful menstruation, bloating, headaches, and can bring on a delayed or infrequent period. Good for maintaining uterus health.

Burdock

Common Name: Burdock
Latin Name: Arctium lappa
Plant family: Asteraceae/Compositae (daisy family)
Common parts used: root, leaf, and seeds
Actions: alterative, diaphoretic, diuretic, urinary tonic
Energetics: bitter, cooling, sweet

Description: Biennial that grows up to two meters high and just as wide. Green leaves with reddish stalks and whitish undersides. The seedpods are burrs. Burrs are what Velcro was invented from. The bur, in burdock, is named after the burrs.

Uses (common and uncommon): Burdock is a blood cleaning and purifying liver tonic. Through aiding the liver, burdock supports the lymphatic system. Can help alleviate health ailments associated with heat and hot outbursts, such as cysts. Contains large amounts of iron, vitamin C, and inulin. Good overall health tonic.

Used internally and externally, burdock root is good for skin problems such as teenage acne, menstrual pimples, eczema, rashes, and cysts. Good for inflammatory ailments such as muscle disease. Burdock has blood sugar lowering effects and is used in helping to manage blood sugar levels in diabetes. Help with hay fever.

Safety Issues and Precautions: Non-toxic. May cause severe allergic reaction if you have sensitivity to the Asteraceae/Compositae family, which includes ragweed, chrysanthemums, marigolds and daisies, among others. Consult a doctor before using burdock if you have diabetes as it may lower blood sugar levels too far. Also, consult a herbalist before using when pregnant or breastfeeding.

Planting/Growing: Likes fertile soil. Found growing in ditches and on roadsides.

Harvesting: Best to harvest at the end of the first year, before it has gone to seed in the second year. When the plant goes to seed, it takes the energy from the roots and directs it into the seed. The first frost sends the energy into the roots for the winter. Use a Garden Fork to loosen up the soil around its deep roots. Roots can grow as far down as the plant grows up. Using a garden fork will help you avoid cutting through the lateral roots.

Menstruation notation: A liver aid is good for the female reproductive system because it helps regulate hormone production, which helps bloating, PMS, breast tenderness, menstrual acne, and sporadic periods.

Chaste Tree

Common Name: Chaste tree
Latin Name: Vitex agnus-castus
Plant family: Lamiaceae
Common parts used: berry
Actions: astringent, cephalic, emmenagogue, nervine
Energetics: cooling

Description: Known as a 'woman's herb.' This shrub grows up to 7 meters tall and has palm-shaped leaves with small light purple flowers that make purple berries.

Uses (common and uncommon): A uterine tonic. Chaste tree berry is used for PMS, menstrual cramps, irregular menstruation, breast pain, and acne from hormonal imbalances in women and teenagers, and recovery from birth control pills.

Increases lactation in nursing mothers. Helps with the symptoms of menopause.

Safety Issues and Precautions: Generally safe. Avoid use during pregnancy and consult a health practitioner if using hormonal contraceptives.

Planting/Growing: These shrubs enjoy lots of sun and well-drained soil.

Harvesting: Collect the berries when they are ripe to the point of almost being brown.

Menstruation notation: Used for PMS, menstrual cramps, irregular menstruation, breast pain, acne from hormonal imbalances in women and teenagers, and recovery from birth control pills.

 Cramp Bark

Common Name: Cramp Bark
Latin Name: Viburnum opulus
Plant family: Caprifoliaceae
Common parts used: bark, young stems, and root bark
Actions: anti-inflammatory, antispasmodic, astringent, emmenagogue, nervine
Energetics: bitter, cooling, drying

Description: A women's herb known best for its ability as a uterine nervine and for preventing miscarriage due to stress. A deciduous perennial shrub that grows to 13 feet tall with white flowers and then red berries.

Uses (common and uncommon): An excellent herb to relax the uterine muscles. It relieves muscle spasms and has a sedating effect on the reproductive system. This uterine nervine is used to prevent miscarriage. The threatened miscarriage may be due to stress, tension, anxiety, stress of the nerves and uterine tension.

A preventative medicine and remedy for menstrual cramps. A tonic for excessive menstrual bleeding: long and/or heavy cycles, cycles that come twice a month or excessive bleeding during menopause.

Safety Issues and Precautions/ Medication Interactions: No known side effects. Non-toxic.

Planting/Growing: Grows wild. Enjoys moist, rich, loamy soil. Grows in woodlands, hedges and prefers full sun. Can grow from seed or cuttings.

Harvesting: Collect the bark in spring and summer on a dry day while the plant is flowering. Or in the autumn while the bark is easier to remove before the buds begin growing again.

Menstruation notation: Use for excessive menstrual bleeding. Used to prevent and remedy cramps.

Dandelion

Common Name: Dandelion
Latin Name: Taraxacum officinale
Plant family: Asteraceae/Compositae (daisy family)
Common parts used: root, leaf, and flowers
Actions: cholagogue, diuretic, hepatic, mild laxative, sto-

machic, tonic
Energetics: bitter, cooling, drying

Description: The common yellow dandelion is an old and popular perennial herb. While often seen as short, having been trimmed into a bonsai- like plant by lawnmowers and landscaping, dandelions can grow up to two inches wide by 18 inches tall. A bitter taproot with jagged green leaves and a yellow flower that turns into little white helicopter puffs when gone to seed. The seeds disperse in the wind. The roots and stem have bitter white milk inside you can see by breaking either.

Uses (common and uncommon): A great kidney, liver and endocrine gland tonic. Used for cleaning metabolic waste through the blood. Helps with biliary problems and skin problems. Can be used to help gallstones. It is anti-rheumatic. Good for degenerative joint disorders and lowering blood cholesterol. Good for digestive upsets. The leaf helps with menstrual bloating, PMS and breast tenderness. The root, a great liver tonic, helps regulate hormone production.

Safety Issues and Precautions: No known toxicity. Dandelion leaf is one of the safest diuretics available.

Planting/Growing: This common weed grows wild and can be found anywhere grass grows. The wind-carried seeds end up everywhere the wind blows, including garden beds where they are easiest and safest to harvest. This plant grows larger leaves when there is tall grass around it.

Harvesting: Harvest leaves in the spring when they're less bitter and easier to eat. Harvest the roots in the autumn after the flowers have gone to seed or died back. Use a shovel to dig down at least 10 inches to harvest the dandelions taproot. Look for clean plants, especially when harvesting the greens. Harvesting from gardens is easiest because the soil has been worked and doesn't take as much effort to pry from the ground. Avoid harvesting from roadsides where plants accumulate exhaust from vehicles.

Menstruation notation: A liver aid is good for the female reproductive system because it helps regulate hormone production, which helps bloating, PMS, breast tenderness, menstrual acne, and sporadic periods. High iron helps if one is constantly tired and stressed or anemic.

Common Name: Dong Quai
Latin Name: Angelica sinensis
Plant family: Umbelliferae
Common parts used: root
Actions: tonic, analgesic, antispasmodic, diaphoretic, emmenagogue, rejuvenating
Energetics: heating, pungent, sweet

Description: One of the known female herbs, also called 'Angelica,' and known as the 'female ginseng.' A perennial that grows up to three feet tall and flowers in the autumn with a five-petal white flower that forms into an umbrella-like form.

Uses (common and uncommon): As a uterine tonic, and great woman's herb, it helps regulate the menstrual cycle. Used for strengthening the uterus, it is an aid for menstrual problems, such as dysmenorrhea and irregular periods that don't come every cycle or at all. It is also used to bring on periods and regulate them. Dong Quai may bring on bleeding and shouldn't be used while on your period.

Good for the liver and endocrine system. An aid for normalizing hormones and for skin problems. Dong Quai can be used internally or externally to help the skin. Can help with rheumatism.

Safety Issues and Precautions/ Medication Interactions: Non-toxic and safe to take over a long period of time. Avoid using while on your period or while pregnant as it may stimulate bleeding. Use only in combination with other herbs. Avoid using if you are taking blood-thinning medication or have a blood clotting disorder. Dong Quai can be confused with poison hemlock, which is poisonous. Be careful to properly identify your plant.

Planting/Growing: Prefers moist soil and likes semi-shade.

Harvesting: Best to harvest the roots in the autumn after the flowers have died back.

Menstruation notation: Helps to regulate the menstrual cycle, strengthen the uterus and regulate periods of young women in the beginning year of their menstrual cycles. The 'bringing on of the period' should be achieved by taking this herb in the weeks leading up to a period, but not during the period, and then again used after the period has finished and come to a complete cycle.

Evening Primrose

Common Name: Evening Primrose (Oil)
Latin Name: Oenothera birnnis
Plant family: Onagraceae
Common parts used: seed (oil is made from the seeds)

Actions: antidepressant, antispasmodic, anti-inflammatory, nervine, relaxant, vulnerary
Energetics: moistening, neutral

Description: A beautiful yellow flower named after the evening time when its petals open up to be pollinated by moths. A biennial that grows as high as 3 meters. This plant has a main stem that grows from its taproot. Blooms in early summer and the yellow flowers turn to pods of brown seeds. The oil is made from the seeds and can be taken as a supplement found in health stores. It is an ingredient often found in menstruation medications or herbal healing combinations. High in gamma-linolenic acid and omega 3 and 6 essential fatty acids.

Uses (common and uncommon): Good for women's issues: PMS, mood swings, cramps, delayed or irregular periods, and especially good for treating endometriosis. Helps with acne, atopic eczema, skin problems and headaches.

Used to treat nerve damage caused by diabetes, rheumatoid arthritis, neuralgia, chronic fatigue syndrome and alcoholism. Helpful in treating obesity. Must take over a long period of time for the herb to be the most effective.

Safety Issues and Precautions: Safe. Avoid using or consult a physician if you have mania, epilepsy or are considering using evening primrose oil while taking corticosteroids, phenothiazines, non-steroidal anti-inflammatory drugs. Do not take evening primrose oil if you are on medications that slow blood clotting, like anticoagulants, aspirin or Advil. Consult a physician if you are unsure.

Planting/Growing: Grows in poor soils, loamy, just needs full sun.

Harvesting: Seedpods ripen in the autumn, but to get the oil, buy it from a health food store. It's almost impossible to extract the oil from these very small seeds by yourself.

Menstruation notation: Good for PMS, mood swings, cramps, acne, delayed and irregular periods.

Licorice

Common Name: Licorice
Latin Name: Glycyrrhiza glabra
Plant family: Leguminosae/Fabaceae (pea and bean family)
Common parts used: root and rhizome
Actions: demulcent, expectorant, tonic, rejuvenation, laxative, sedative, emetic
Energetics: sweet, bitter, cooling

Description: Perennial shrub that grows from one to two meters high. Dark green pinnate leaves with purple flowers. Licorice grows a taproot with runners. Medicinal herb used for its sweetness and to sweeten other herbal mixtures making them more tasty and easy to eat.

Uses (common and uncommon): A smooth sweet tasting herb that is medicinal on its own but is also used in combination to sweeten the taste of other medicines. An anti-inflammatory used for respiratory problems like coughs, colds and bronchitis. Good for the endocrine system, reproductive system and hormone regulation. Considered to be estrogen stimulating. An adrenal tonic. A calming restorative food that nourishes the spirit and the brain. Relieves muscle spasms and improves voice by bringing strength to the vocal cords. Improves vision, hair and complexion. Can be taken as tea, fresh or dried, or the root can be chewed on as is.

Safety Issues and Precautions: Licorice root is generally safe and has long been used as a medicine. May cause water retention and inhibit the absorption of calcium. Don't take if you are pregnant or have osteoporosis, heart disease, hormone-sensitive conditions, hypertonia, hypokalemia (low potassium levels in the blood) and/or kidney disease.

Planting/Growing: Often cultivated and sometimes wild, enjoys well-drained soil in full sun.

Harvesting: When the plant is at least three years old, the roots will be big enough to start harvesting. In the autumn after the leaves die back, using a spade or shovel, dig around the plant until you can see the roots to remove the plant. Leave some of the roots so they grow new plants.

Menstruation notation: Regulates hormones and strengthens the endocrine system.

Common Name: Nettle
Latin Name: Urtica dioica
Plant family: Urticaceae
Common parts used: Leaves, stalk, roots
Actions: alterative, astringent, depurative, diuretic, hypotensive, laxative, tonic
Energetics: cooling, drying

Description: Also known as 'stinging nettles.' This plant has small fine hairs covering the leaves and stalks that sting like little bees or ants. The sting can be felt for a few minutes to a few hours or longer while red spreads from the sting where the nettles get in your skin. This plant grows up to six feet tall and its opposing leaves have serrated edges. Nettle is one of the highest sources of digestible iron.

Uses (common and uncommon): Nettle is a food; also called 'wild spinach' that is an excellent source of digestible iron. When the plant is cooked, the stinging hairs soften and become edible. Used for anemia and menstrual difficulties, a great liver, blood and endocrine tonic high in calcium, Vitamin A, K and chlorophyll.

Good for urinary problems. The Greek name for nettle 'uro' means urine because nettle is good for the kidneys. Nettle root is a tonic for the genitourinary system (the genital and urinary organs) and is good as a prostate tonic. Helpful with respiratory and digestive issues and can help with hay fever and other allergies. A safe and nourishing herb for pregnant and breastfeeding women.

The little stingers on the plant are good for arthritis and rheumatism when stung. Good for gout and joints.

Safety Issues and Precautions: The nettle sting is more powerful than it appears. Don't forget to use gloves when touching the plant. Stingers are all over, and one can easily forget by looking at it. Not to be eaten raw! Not a salad green.

Planting/Growing: Grows wild. Likes rich wet soil.

Harvesting: Harvest in the spring. Collect the new growth on top. Cut the bud looking section in the middle on top and one or two sets of opposing leaves underneath, so the plant has a chance to replenish itself. Wearing gloves is the best way to handle nettles. Use scissors to snip the stem and catch your harvest in a bag, box or bowl.

Menstruation notation: A liver aid is good for the female reproductive system because it helps regulate hormone production, which helps bloating, PMS, breast tenderness, menstrual acne, and sporadic periods. High iron helps if one is constantly tired and stressed or anemic.

Oregon Grape Root

Common Name: Oregon Grape
Latin Name: Mahonia aquafolium
Plant family: Berberidaceae
Common parts used: root
Actions: alterative, antimicrobial, antipyretic, laxative, tonic
Energetics: bitter, cooling, drying

Description: An evergreen shrub that's leaves look like holly with little yellow flowers that bloom in the spring. It can grow up to six feet tall and just as wide. This is the official state flower of Oregon. It isn't a true grape but has grape-like fruits. This liver aid can be found as a supplement if it doesn't grow close to you.

Uses (common and uncommon): A liver aid used to move stagnancy out. Stimulates bile production and can help get you started if you plan to loose weight. Helps to digest fat and oils and regulate the menstrual cycle.

Safety Issues and Precautions: Avoid use during pregnancy.

Planting/Growing: Grows wild. An evergreen shrub that

grows in the Pacific Northwest. Grows well in richly acidic, well-drained soil in partial shade.

Harvesting: Root and rhizome are harvested in the autumn. Watch out for prickly leaves when getting around the plant.

Menstruation notation: Helps to regulate the menstrual cycle.

Raspberry Leaf

Common Name: Red Raspberry
Latin Name: Rubus idaeus
Plant family: Rosaceae
Common parts used: leaf
Actions: astringent, alterative, antiemetic, hemostatic, parturient, refrigerant, tonic
Energetics: astringent, cooling, sweet

Description: Red raspberry leaf is known as a 'pregnancy and birth herb.' The raspberry plant is a shrub that grows up to two meters tall with prickly stems, smallish green leaves, and sweet red berries. And though you can use the common and easily identifiable raspberry plant, the wild raspberry plant (that grows wild) is more potent.

Uses (common and uncommon): Used as an aid in pregnancy and in childbirth to ease labor pains. Raspberry leaf can be used for the entire nine months of pregnancy. After birth, it helps to restore the reproductive system and build a healthy milk supply. Used to ease morning sickness and nausea, and prevent miscarriage in pregnant women. Red raspberry leaf is a uterine tonic that tones and relaxes the uterine muscles and firms the pelvic muscles during pregnancy. Stops hemorrhaging, excessive bleeding and excessive menstruation. Good if your periods are running long and/or heavy.

High in calcium and iron. Supplies extra calcium and iron during pregnancy, and builds bones and teeth. A remedy for fevers, diarrhea, and dysentery. Can be used for yeast and colon health, heartburn and ulcers.

Safety Issues and Precautions: No residual side effects, considered a safe herb.

Planting/Growing: Raspberry plants are sold and grown as canes. When growing raspberries, they like rich well-drained soil. To be planted from November to March.

Harvesting: Pick leaves in the spring before the plant has flowered. Cut the young bright green leaves at the tops of the stems. Be careful of the prickly thorns when cutting the new growth.

Menstruation notation: Stops hemorrhaging. Good herb to take if you have long periods and/or excessive bleeding during menstruation.

Valerian

Common Name: Valerian
Latin Name: Valeriana officinalis
Plant family: Caprifoliaceae (honeysuckle family)
Common parts used: root
Actions: antispasmodic, emmenagogue, hypnotic, hypoten-

sive, nervine, sedative, tonic
Energetics: bitter, drying, warming

Description: Known as the herb for nervous stress and tension. A white flowering plant that grows up to two feet high. This perennial has a pungent odor that smells of 'smelly socks' but luckily doesn't taste like it.

Uses (common and uncommon): A mild sedative. A recommended herb for insomnia, stress and the nervous system. Helps with headaches, reducing pain, anxiety, sleep and nervous system disorders. An ingredient used in over-the-counter drugs. A medicine for tension, irritability, hypertension and stress-related heart problems. Helpful to take for poor blood circulation. Can be taken internally and externally as a bath.

A uterine tonic with muscle relaxant properties that helps relieve menstrual tension and stress.

Safety Issues and Precautions: Safe and non-addictive. May cause a foggy head or slow complex thoughts up to a few hours after consumption. Avoid use during pregnancy or when breastfeeding. Do not mix with alcohol, Xanax, benzodiazepines or central nervous system suppressant medication. Consult a physician if you are unsure about what medications you are taking or if there is any conflict.

Planting/Growing: Enjoys rich well-drained nitrogenized soil in full sun. To grow a larger root, cut the flower stalks off to send more energy to the root. Water heavily and infrequently.

Harvesting: Harvest in autumn or the early spring using a spade or garden fork.

Menstruation notation: Helps alleviate menstrual tension and stress.

Yellow Dock

Common Name: Yellow Dock
Latin Name: Rumex crispus
Plant family: Polygonaceae
Common parts used: root
Actions: alterative, antipyretic, astringent, laxative
Energetics: bitter, cooling, pungent

Description: A great liver tonic. Yellow dock is a perennial flowering plant with green petal-less flowers with a touch of red. Grows up to 1.5 meters tall and the leaves are slightly curled around the edges. It's sometimes called the 'curly dock' to differentiate it from other types of dock.

Uses (common and uncommon): Liver stimulant, detoxifier and cleanser. Cleans and enriches blood. Mineral rich and high in iron, yellow dock helps build blood and can be used to treat anemia. Good for the endocrine system. Great for skin problems and can treat oily skin. Helps to reduce pain and inflammation. Aids in weight loss through the digestion of fats and oils. Helps with cerebral circulation.

Safety Issues and Precautions: Do not use if emaciated.

Planting/Growing: Grows wild. Often found on roadsides or in fields.

Harvesting: The root is a yellowish brown color. When dug up, the root is straight, up to a length of twelve inches long.

Menstruation notation: A liver aid is good for the female reproductive system because it helps regulate hormone production, which helps bloating, PMS, breast tenderness, menstrual acne, and sporadic periods. High iron helps if one is constantly tired and stressed or anemic.

Online Resources

General

My Beautiful Cervix
http://www.beautifulcervix.com
Real live pictures of a cervix through an entire cycle that give a visual to cervical fluid and period blood. Before viewing remind yourself that they're real live pictures, not illustrations.
Age: All- with comfort seeing blood and gooey pictures

Our Bodies Ourselves
http://www.ourbodiesourselves.org
Lots of body-oriented information and sex education

Scarleteen
http://www.scarleteen.com
If you've have started having sex or are interested in starting, it is a wealth of sexuality information.
Age: Teens +

Shameless Magazine
http://www.shamelessmag.com
A magazine for girls and trans youth based out of Toronto, Canada, website featuring articles.
Age: Teens +

Kids Health
http://www.kidshealth.org
Website available in Spanish
Age: Kids, teens, parents and educators

U by Kotex
http://www.ubykotex.com
Puberty and your period
Run by Kotex Australia
Age: Kids and teens

Kids Help Phone
1-800-668-6868, http://www.kidshelpphone.ca
Kids Help Phone is Canada's only free, national, bilingual, confidential and anonymous, 24-hour telephone and online counselling service.
Age: Kids and teens

Feminine Care Products

These sites may include free samples for collect for part of you testing as well as useful information on taking care of your body, and of course, the items they sell.

Diva Cup
http://www.divacup.com
The most popular reusable menstrual cup on the market

Eco Femme
http://ecofemme.org/
A new design of cloth pads and cloth pieces

GladRags
http://gladrags.com/
Find the Sea Sponge here as well as cloth pads

Lunapads
http://www.lunapads.com
Cloth pads with great design

Natracare
http://www.natracare.com
Organic disposable pads and tampons

Reproduction

Planned Parenthood
Plannedparenthood.org
Abortion information, birth alternatives and statistics, birth control

Sexualityandu.ca
This website is managed by The Society of Obstetricians and Gynaecologists of Canada (SOGC). Includes a wide variety of information on birth control, STIs- STDs and sexual health.

OPT Options for Sexual Health
http://www.sexualhealth.org
Sexual health educators answering questions and birth control resources

Sex, Etc.
http://www.sexetc.com
Sex education for teens by teens

Charting: Help For Tracking Changes

Free Apps

Period Tracker Lite by GP Apps
Compatibility: Requires iOS 4.3 or later. Compatible with iPhone, iPad, and iPod touch. This app is optimized for iPhone 5.
Age: 12 +

Period Plus (Menstrual, Fertile, Ovulation Calendar, Tracker, Affirmations & POPSUGAR for Women Cycle) Compatibility: Requires iOS 5.0 or later. Compatible with iPhone, iPad, and iPod touch. This app is optimized for iPhone 5.

Moon Charting

Menstruation
http://www.menstruation.com.au
Charting your cycle with the moon

Moon Mysteries
http://www.moonmysteries.com/moon-cycle-chart
How to use a moon cycle chart

For Information On The Moon

Old Farmers Almanac
http://www.oldfarmersalmanac.com/moon

Heritage and Heirloom Seeds

Places to buy these seeds, like seed banks and seed companies are popping up all over the globe. Search one closest to you or check out these which are just a few.

Canada
Salt Spring Seeds
http://www.saltspringseeds.com
West Coast Seeds
https://www.westcoastseeds.com

United States
Seed Savers Exchange
http://www.seedsavers.org
Johnny Seeds
http://www.johnnyseeds.com

Bibliography and Notes

Chapter 1: The Secret
Melchizedek, D. (1999). The Ancient Secret of the Flower of Life. Flagstaff, Arizona: Light Technology Publishing.

Chapter 3: Flower of Life
Norsigian, J., & Boston Women's Health Book Collective. (2011). Our Bodies, Ourselves. New York: Touchstone, p. 228-38.

> *You will find new and clear updated information on all women's issues and information concerned a woman's body.*

Northrup, C. (2010). Women's Bodies, Women's Wisdom. New York: Bantam Books, p. 234, 258-66.

> *Christiane Northrup writes on the gamut of women's issues including but not limited to menstrual cycles, feelings and emotions, energy healing, disease, abortion and is famous for finding the parallels in women's speech, thought, action and physical conditions. Northrup is a M.D. and has spoken on how women embody feelings and beliefs in each aspect of their lives into their physical bodies and as a result have physical ailments.*

Weschler, T. (2006). Taking Charge Of Your Fertility 10th Anniversary Edition: The Definitive Guide to Natural Birth Control. New York.

> *This author provides extensive information on cervical fluid including illustrations for many possible textures through one's entire cycle.*

Chapter 4: Reproductive Cycle
Norsigian, Our Bodies, Ourselves, p. 240
Northrup, Women's Bodies, p. 99-163.

Chapter 5: Moon Time
Olson, D. W., Flenberg, R. T., & Sinnott, R. (2006, 07 27). What's a Blue Moon? Sky and Telescope. Accessed at http://www.skyandtelescope.com/observing/objects/moon/3304131.html on June 23, 2015

> *Sky and Telescope published the original article on What's a Blue Moon and it was taken out of context and cited in many books which is how, as it's stated in the article, The Blue Moon became known as the second blue moon in a month. This article clarifies all pertinent information regarding the 'Blue Moon'.*

Chapter 7: Nature's Medicine Cabinet
Gladstar, R. (1993). Herbal Healing for Women. New York: Fireside, p. 77, 79-83, 92.

> *Renowned herbalist for women's health, in this book you will find practical herbal lessons and solutions for common female health issues.*

Ober, C., Sinatra, Stephen T., Zucker, M. (2014). Earthing: The most important health discovery ever. CA: Basic Health Publications, Inc, p. 180, 184-190.

Tomkins, P., & Bird, C. (1989). The Secret Life of Plants: A fascinating account of the physical, emotional, and spiritual relations between plants and man. New York: Harper Perennial.

> *An oldie but a goodie. This will open you up to a whole new world of plant understanding, a new relationship with the world that surrounds us as we are in particular need of as they provide us with surprising health benefits.*

Turner, N. (2011). The Hormone Diet: A 3-Step Program to Help You Lose Weight, Gain Strength, and Live Younger Longer. New York: Rondale Books.

> *The title may read as though this is a diet book but rest assured it's the least likely to suggest you diet. Hormones are carefully explained as the source of feelings, how they function and how they react to what we put inside us. A resource for bearing in mind what you eat affects not only your body but also your feelings.*

Chapter 8: How Your Mother Got Pregnant

Melchizedek, Ancient Secret of the Flower of Life, p. 184- 89.

Chapter 9: Birth Control

Myss, C. (1996). Anatomy of the Spirit. New York: Three Rivers Press, p. 132-42.

> The Power of Choice including reference to abortion.

Norsigian, Our Bodies, Ourselves, p. 323- 70.

Northrup, Women's Bodies, p. 384- 444.

Weschler, Taking Charge Of Your Fertility 10th Anniversary Edition: The Definitive Guide to Natural Birth Control. p. 116-36.

Chapter 10: Birth

Norsigian, Our Bodies, Ourselves, p. 450-73.

Northrup, Women's Bodies, p. 445-99.

Materia Medica

A Forgotten Tonic Herb: Evening Primrose. (2007). Retrieved March 13, 2016, from http://bearmedicineherbals.com/a-fogotten-tonic-herb-evening-primrose.html

Boon, H., Smith, M., Boon, H., & Boon, H. (2009). 55 most common medicinal herbs: The complete natural medicine guide. Toronto: R. Rose.

Breverton, T., & Culpeper, N. (2011). Breverton's complete herbal: A book of remarkable plants and their uses. Guilford, CT: Lyons Press.

EVENING PRIMROSE OIL: Uses, Side Effects, Interactions and Warnings - WebMD. (n.d.). Retrieved March 13, 2016, from http://www.webmd.com/vitamins-supplements/ingredientmono-1006-evening primrose oil.aspx?activeingredientid=1006

Evening Primrose Oil Benefits & Information (Oenothera Biennis). (n.d.). Retrieved March 13, 2016, from http://www.herbwisdom.com/herb-evening-primrose.html

Flowers, F., Wylde, B., & Ross, S. J. (2014). Power plants: Simple home remedies you can grow. Toronto: Harper Collins.

French Dandelion (Taraxacum officinale vr. sativum). (n.d.). Retrieved April 21, 2016, from http://www.saltspringseeds.com/products/french-dandelion-taraxacum-officinale-vr-sativum

Gladstar, Herbal Healing for Women.

Green, J. (2000). The herbal medicine-makers' handbook: A home manual. Freedom, CA: The Crossing Press.

Lad, V., & Frawley, D. (1986). The yoga of herbs: An Ayurvedic guide to herbal medicine. Santa Fe, NM: Lotus Press.

Rogers, M. (2006). Crampbark [PDF]. Silver Spring, PA: HERBALPEDIA.

Sacred Earth - Foraging: Evening Primrose (Oenothera biennis). (n.d.). Retrieved April 21, 2016, from http://www.sacredearth.com/ethnobotany/foraging/EveningPrimrose.php

Tirtha, S. S. (1998). The Ayurveda encyclopedia: Natural secrets to healing, prevention & longevity. Bayville, NY: Ayurveda Holistic Center Press.

Weed, S. S. (1989). Wise woman herbal healing wise. Woodstock, NY: Ash Tree Pub.

Index

A

Abortion 115–116
Acne 88

B

Basal body temperature 48,
    53, 111
Birth 120–121
Black Cohosh 142
Blood 49–50, 64, 71, 77, 81
Blood fertilizer 80
Blood stains 77–78
Bra fitting 26–28
Breast milk 123–124
Breasts 25–27, 50, 88
Burdock 143

C

Cervical fluid 37, 53
Cervix 37–40, 45, 49, 70, 118,
    122
Chaste Tree 145
Choices 115
Clitoris. See Female genitalia
Cloth pads 64, 75, 77
Consensual 102
Cramp Bark 146
Cramps. See Period pains

D

Dandelion 147
Dong Quai 149

E

Earthing 94
Egg 14, 40, 46, 49, 111–112
Evening Primrose 150

F

Feelings 36, 60–61
Female genitalia. See Vulva
    clitoris 34–35
    labia majora 33
    labia minora 33

G

Grounding. See Earthing

H

Herbal supplements 95
Herb garden 86
Hormones 112
Hymen 35, 72

L

Labia. See Female genitalia
Licorice 152

M

Materia Medica 141
Menstrual cycle. See Reproductive
    cycle
Menstrual pads

cloth 75
disposable 68
Moon
blue moon 57
moon time 54–56
Morning after pill 116
Mound of venus 34

N

Natural Birth Control 113
Natural birth control methods 113
Nettles 153

O

Oregon Grape Root 155
Ovum. *See* Egg

P

Pads 66, 75, 77
Pee hole. *See* Urethra
Period pains 90
Period shame 52
Plant medicine 83–88, 94–97
PMS 88, 90, 94–96
Pregnancy 119–121
Pre-Menstrual Syndrome. *See* PMS
Privacy 88
Puberty
pubic hair 30

R

Raspberry Leaf 156
Reproductive cycle 81
Reproductive system 41–53
cervix 37, 37–39
fallopian tubes 40

ovaries 40
Rose hips 86

S

Sea sponge 78
Semen 107
Sensitive breasts 88
Sex 101–106
Sperm 49, 107, 111–113
Spirit 124
STDs. *See* STIs
STIs 112, 117

T

Tampon
first time 68
with applicator 74

U

Urethra 35

V

Vagina 37–38
Valerian 157
Vulva 24, 30, 33–36, 65, 104

Y

Yellow Dock 159
Yoni 70

CPSIA information can be obtained
at www.ICGtesting.com
Printed in the USA
LVOW06s0736311216
519346LV00004B/6/P